Carrie

Season of a Second Chance

Based on a true story

By Dorothy J. Lyons

Carrie
by Dorothy Lyons

Printed in the United States of America

ISBN 1-59781-237-4

www.xulonpress.com

2006

Introduction

It was a perfect, summer day and *she* was standing at the front door of her little house, waving goodbye. We had just enjoyed one of my Mom's family dinners. Her good *Southern* cooking is always a treat. The sunlight was shining on her face, making her snow-white hair gleam.

I had seen her standing *there* so many times before, wistfully waving, as we were leaving to go back to our lives. The look on her face was so familiar. However, on this particular day, as I looked back to return her wave, the scene suddenly changed and I saw myself standing in *her* place.

Welling up inside of me I felt a pride.....the warm feeling of family and the love I have for my Mom. I could see the nostalgia in her expression and I, myself, began to feel the special kind of loneliness, that must have produced the weak smile on her face. I saw, in her, the resignation that time marches on....passing you by.

It occurred to me, that I also had begun to perform the same task of waving, as my own children, with their families, disappeared around the corner in the road. Only then could I pull myself away to return inside and close the door.

The years are going by ....and old age is not *that* far

away. Memories are all *I* have now of the hard work and sacrifice, the joys of babyhood, the rigors of childhood and the trials of the teenage years.

However, there is a reward. A certain pride you feel as *your* children assume adulthood and begin to raise a family of their own.

Like every other person, there was a time I thought I knew it all. Following us, our own children thought they knew much more than we could possibly know and some day their children will feel the same.

Those of you with young children, take heart. From my own experience, I find, gratefully, that somewhere around their twenty-fifth birthday and having a child of their own, they realize that they *may* still have something to learn.

The sight of my mother standing in her doorway, watching us leave, produced in me a soul-stirring experience. I *always* turn to wave goodbye, one last time, just to let her know that I care. On that day, as well, I started thinking about her life.

Just who is she? What joys and sorrows has she experienced and what has her life meant to her.....as well as to her family and others?

Two years ago my brothers, sisters and I, celebrated my mom's eightieth birthday. We had a wonderful party and the whole family attended. There were children and grandchildren, great-grand children, sons- in- law and grandsons- in –law; daughters-in law and granddaughters-in law. Even her brother and sisters, who were *all* still living, came to celebrate. Everyone was there. It was a truly special occasion, for her and for us. She was and is a great mom!

As I drove away, I knew that I wanted to leave her a special *legacy*. Something, from which my children and their children could profit. It is the story of *her* unmovable hope!

Her life, though simple by the worlds standard, has not

been lived in vain. Neither is *our* life in vain. God had a plan for her and He has a plan for all of us, if we listen. If we fail to fulfill His plan in any way.....it is good to know that God gives us second chances to redeem our lives *and* our souls.

"Carrie" ***Season of a Second Chance*** is about my Mom, my friend and my teacher.

Through her life, determination and most of all, her faith in God, I found a basis of how to live a life that makes memories. In the midst of trouble, it also provides a strong building block, which is the foundation of family and faith.....on which I continue to build. I pray my own children, with God's help, will do the same.

I dedicate this book to my Mom and *my* four wonderful children.

Thank you Mom, because you unknowingly gave me information for this book. I also want to thank my sisters who provided input from their perspective. And, my brothers.

Most of all, to *you*, the reader, may this book provide new hope if *your* hope is failing and provide confirmation, if it is needed, that *your* life is not in vain.

God is truly the God of second chances.

Dorothy

Chapter One

The hot, Alabama sun was unrelenting as little Carrie, struggled to drag the well-worn muslin bag behind her. It would hold one-hundred pounds of cotton when full.

"I'm almost finished," she thought.

The sun, which had been unmerciful in its attack, was now beginning its final descent. It would soon disappear behind the trees, in the distant meadow, leaving a beautiful multicolored glow in the sky.

"Whew!" Carrie sighed softly, as she took a deep breath and wiped the damp hair from her brow. As she looked again toward the meadow, she saw the sun slowly pass from view.

The daily sunsets provided a lovely picture and she loved the array of colors. As she paused to take in the sight, she could imagine herself painting the beautiful picture.

Carrie, liked playing in the green meadow, which lay just beyond those trees, when there was time for such a luxury and she willingly let her mind carry her there.

Her brother's call to her, that it was time to stop working for the day, jarred her from the momentary daydream and back to reality. Carrie, feeling surprisingly weary, began to walk down the neat rows of cotton stalks to see what verdict the old, rusty, cotton scale would produce.

Long before daybreak, she began her work. She had endured the pricks of the cotton bolls, the teasing of her older brother and the unpredictable antics of her younger sisters.

A gentle slap on the back, from Papa Ed, made her painfully aware of the sunburn which was inevitable on her fair skin.

She had worked with purpose to reach her goal.....one-hundred pounds of cotton, which she alone had picked, in one day's time.

Picking cotton was not new for Carrie. Working in the dusty fields, harvesting the crop of the season, was a daily routine. However, on this day it was different. She was working for something special!

Tears began to sting her lovely brown eyes as dusk set in and she realized the day was gone. She had not yet reached her goal.

* * *

Eva, Carrie's mom, had quit work in the fields earlier in the day and by this time, had been in the kitchen for a couple of hours preparing the evening meal. Corn bread and a variety of vegetables were cooking on their wood-burning stove. The squash and greens she had picked earlier that day, choosing from the crops that were considered *seconds,* was ample fare. The best crops were for market of course, because they brought the *best price*.

The family of eight children, four from Papa Ed's first marriage and four from Mama Eva's first marriage, were responsible to make their living as itinerant farmers.

The Chamberlains moved every year to another farm, where they began anew to carve out a life for themselves in the red clay, or possibly the sandy loam, of southern Alabama.

The children attended school when they could, but the crops always took priority. This was not out of the ordinary for the Chamberlain family, or the other surrounding farmers. Making a living was a family affair and everyone had to do his or her share, according to their age or capability.

The time was 1930 and Carrie, within a few days, would be eight-years-old. She was the second oldest of her mother, Eva's children and the oldest girl. This automatically brought with it the responsibility of sometimes being *the mom*, even at her tender age. Carrie, was a quiet girl with a somewhat serious side and a rare hint of humor. She was very shy and inward which made her, at times, somewhat of a mystery.

Her sisters Maggie, now six-years-old and Hazel, four-years-old, were the more carefree members of the family. Not just because of their age, but their personalities as well. Their attention span was very short at those tender ages. You could find the two of them tumbling in the tall grass, playing with each other as contagious giggles echoed across the fields. They too worked with the family learning responsibility, but they were both given easier tasks.

Carrie's brother, Jeffery, was two years older than she was. At age ten, he was a mild-mannered boy with a nice smile and wavy reddish-brown hair. He was also designated guardian of his younger sisters when Mama Eva was busy in the fields, or away in town working at the sewing factory.

Today, he was keeping an eye on Hazel and Maggie because Carrie, had made it clear to him that she was going to be too busy to chase after them.

The Chamberlain family found life on the farm hard, but not without its rewards. This was a period in time, when neighbors were truly neighbors and did not mind leading a hand. They shared their joys and defeats and really got to know each other.

Their social times consisted of peanut shellings, quilting bees, and Saturday night trips in the wagon, through the woods....... to visit their friends or family at a nearby farm. These were cherished times indeed and they would be engraved in their memories forever.

* * *

The Chamberlains were a religious family and attended church on Sunday, when the farm chores permitted. Eva Chamberlain had depended on this spiritual strength to see her through the times of sadness, which she had experienced early in her life.

Eva, married Ed Chamberlain a couple of years before, more as a matter of necessity. She was a young woman in her late twenties with a pretty round face, fine brown hair drawn up in a roll at the nape of her neck, and slight of build. She was very handy with the sewing machine and made her own clothes, as well as her children's, from flour sacks. When the sacks were empty and washed the patterned cloth made suitable material. Eva, was very good at making patterns and dying the sackcloth to the color she wanted the clothing to be. She seldom had a pattern but her own imagination and talent was all she needed.

When Eva Jennings, met Ed Chamberlain, she was a young widow with four small children. Her husband, Frank, had died from a rare blood disease, when Carrie was almost seven-years-old. Eva, cared a great deal for Ed. He was a very pleasing man with dark hair, olive skin and quite a bit taller than she. However, Carrie's father, Frank Jennings, was Eva's young and handsome "first love," so gentle in nature....with a fun loving disposition. She still missed him deeply.

Carrie and Jeffery, were barely old enough when their father died to remember much about him. They remember mostly, that he was a kind man with sandy-auburn hair. Jeffery, had inherited his father's auburn hair as well as his gentle disposition.

* * *

Papa Ed's wife had died, a few years before, also leaving him with four young children. The two boys and two girls were a little older than their new stepbrother and sisters, Jeffery, Carrie, Maggie and Hazel. However, the children soon adapted and became more like real brothers and sisters. In fact, if you did not know otherwise, you would think that the eight children, descending like doorsteps in age, *were* blood brothers and sisters.

Ed and Eva, worked side by side to give *all* of the children the best life they could, as they blended their lives together in work, love, sacrifice, and faith.

* * *

It was the 1930's and the great depression made life hard for everyone. Even the very rich were not exempt. The big, stock market crash of the late twenties had paralyzed the country.

The *crash* was worse on those who lost large fortunes, because they did not know how to "make do" with *just a little*, like the poorest people did.

Stories were told of many people committing suicide, or becoming beggars and drunks, trying to come to terms with what life had dealt them. Some, could *not* endure the poverty...... thrust on them so quickly and chose to end their own lives, either literally or figuratively.

The Chamberlain family.... and others like them, just kept on doing what they knew to do....farming.

* * *

The hottest part of the day was gone but it left Carrie tired and quite disappointed as she continued to drag the heavy bag of cotton, in an almost futile effort. She finally enlisted Jeffery's help to drag it the last few yards, to the fence, where her *final* bag of cotton would be weighed.

"Oh.....Just as I thought," muttered Carrie disappointedly, as Papa Ed swung the bag up and the scale adjusted. Her accumulated total for the day was only ninety-pounds. She was ten pounds short of her goal.

Carrie's face fell in disappointment as her mind pictured the coveted watch, in the window of Mr. Dayton's general store just a few miles away. She *really* wanted that watch!

A family friend had seen her admiring the toy watch just a few days before and he had promised Carrie that he would buy it for her birthday, *if* she could pick one-hundred pounds of cotton in *one* day.

I don't know if he thought it was not an attainable goal for one so young, or whether he saw a determination in Carrie, that he wanted to challenge. Either way, to Carrie, it was not a game. She wanted that beautiful watch with the single black cord band and the shiny glass stones around the crystal.

* * *

As dusk settled into darkness Mama Eva called her family in for supper. Carrie, sighed audibly trying to absorb the disappointment she felt.

"What's wrong Carrie?" questioned Jeffery.

Carrie, was absorbed in her own thoughts and did not answer him. Walking side by side, they made their way across the spacious back yard to the blue-speckled basin that sat on the back porch. A pitcher of water, drawn from the old well, sat near by on the porch railing. Although tired, they knew that Mama Eva was strict about washing your hands before you sat down to eat at *her* table.

The hungry children quickly found their place around the rough, wooden-slat supper table to enjoy the meal. Mama Eva always made their food very tasty, even if it was considered *seconds.*

Jeffery, talked excitedly about his work that day and he was happy with the fact that he was now spending time with his family. Meal times were a special time of sharing.

Even though he was a quiet-mannered boy, with a gentle spirit, he too was competitive and enjoyed his accomplishment.

The children's sunburned faces became less important as they sat around the table recounting the successes *and* near successes of the day.

Carrie, however, was not very happy. It was obvious to Jeffery that her heart was heavy and neither did her deep disappointment escape Mama Eva's careful eyes.

Hazel and Maggie, kept the scene at the table lively as they giggled at Jeffery's stories and poked food at each other. Carrie, did not participate in the table talk that night, but let her mind drift away, planning how she might *still* reach her goal.

* * *

Carrie, quietly helped Mama Eva with the supper dishes, drying them carefully. Soon, they were placed on the shelves of the open pine cupboard, which was punctuated with a lot of *character marks* received in the yearly moves, from farmhouse to farmhouse, with the Chamberlain family. The cupboard had been Eva's mother's before it was her's and was special, if not beautiful.

As they finished the other evening chores, Mama Eva

tried to comfort Carrie, congratulating her on the cotton she *had* picked that day.....a great accomplishment. Carrie, looked up at Mama Eva giving a consenting smile, but being careful not to give away any signals regarding the plan she had already worked out in her mind.

The Chamberlain family was exhausted from the hot day's work and began to settle down for the night. Papa Ed, sat in his old rocking chair by the fireplace. In the winter, a fire would be burning in the fireplace, fed by pine logs to keep the family warm. August, however, was not the time for a fire. So a metal fire screen, which was once beautiful, but now broken from years of use, hid the fireplace from view.

The Chamberlain family children, climbed into bed, leaving the windows open to let the warm breeze make its way through the wooden-frame house. Of course, the insects also found their way in and could be quite irritating. The mosquitoes were especially plentiful that year.

* * *

The fact that it was a full moon was not lost on Carrie. As she lay in her bed, swatting the bugs and looking out the half-raised window, she could see the fields bathed in the bright glow of moonlight.

As she listened to the *crickets* sing their song, she could still see that *ten-cent watch* in the store window in town. She longed for that treasure to be her own.

* * *

After the house grew quiet and it seemed her family was asleep, the plan that Carrie had been hatching in her mind was soon put in motion.

She climbed from the feather bed that she shared with Maggie, being very careful not to wake her. She slowly slipped on her well-worn denim overalls, which still bore the strong, sweaty smell of the day. Next, she placed the brown, scrappy brogan shoes on her feet. Without socks they had made several blisters on her feet, but they were all she had for working in the field, except for the cloth shoes they occasionally made when *no* shoes were available.

"O-u-c-h," she exclaimed softly, as she pushed the shoes on her bare feet. The blisters, now very sore, made wearing the shoes almost unbearable.

Moving the bedroom door slowly, so it would not squeak, she looked into the parlor to see if Mama Eva and Papa Ed had gone to bed. Seeing no one, she began to make her way softly through the kitchen and outside onto the back porch.

The field was visible only because the moon was so bright. After dark, was certainly not Carrie's favorite time to be outside. In fact, she had a great fear of the darkness. Tonight the moon helped, *a little.*

Passing the back yard fence, she walked carefully, but quickly, down the long rows in the field and found the place where the fluffy, white cotton still stood, shining in the moonlight like homemade ice cream in strangely shaped wooden bowls.

Suddenly feeling pain, she looked down. She could clearly see the pricks, on her fingers, which she had received from picking cotton earlier that day. The cotton bolls could be very sharp and they left her small, tender hands sore to the touch.

She wondered if she would be able to pick the ten-pounds of cotton she needed before her family discovered she was missing. Carrie, quickened her pace and soon arrived at the spot where she had stopped picking earlier in the day.

Driven along, even more by her fear of the dark, Carrie worked as fast as she could and in just a little while had picked enough cotton to finish filling the brown loose-weave sack.

* * *

Maggie, Hazel, and Carrie's two-step sisters, Mary and Ann, slept in the same room with Carrie, due to the lack of space in their modest home, which was provided for them by the owner of the farm.

It was very small, featuring only a parlor, a kitchen and three small bedrooms. One of the bedrooms was on the back of the house, by the porch. That is where Jeffery slept with his two stepbrothers, Evan and Walter.

Jeffery, was having trouble getting to sleep that night as well, and was doing *his* share of watching the bugs fly in the streams of moonlight as it illuminated the fields.

His eyes suddenly caught sight of something which appeared to be an animal moving across the field. After a few moments, his curiosity got the best of him.

"What is that?" he quietly questioned.

He quickly reached for his overalls, made his way onto the back porch and strained to see what was in the distance. Whatever it was, it appeared to be coming closer and he strained even harder to see.

Soon, his eyes fell on Carrie, as she approached the back yard fence.

"What are you doing?" whispered Jeffery, as he ran softly toward her.

"I just had to finish my one-hundred pounds!" Carrie said, panting to catch her breath.

"You could have been hurt you know," Jeffery chastened her, showing momentary concern.

Carrie, admired her brother and she was always on Jeffery's trail. If he was running, she was running. If he was climbing, she was climbing and Jeffery knew his sister could be determined, or *stubborn* as he called it, but he had never seen her quite this determined.

Carrie, stowed the cotton in a safe place for the night, to keep the dew off, and looked toward Jeffery with a big smile. Her face was now shining even brighter than the moonlight. It was almost as bright as that shiny, ten-cent watch she wanted so badly.

Jeffery, knew his mother and Papa Ed would be upset if they discovered Carrie was not in bed and if he told them, Carrie would certainly "be in a heap of trouble."

After Carrie pleaded with him, Jeffery promised not to tell Mama Eva and Papa Ed, in exchange for a favor "at the appropriate time."

Jeffery, made good on his promise, but Mama Eva knew very well that Carrie, had only picked ninety-pounds of cotton that day. When Carrie's cotton was "weighed in" the following day, for the final sale to buyers, it weighed exactly one-hundred pounds.

Mama Eva quickly glanced at Carrie, her eyebrows raised, with a knowing look and a smile playing on her lips, but she did not question how the ninety-pounds mysteriously turned into one-hundred pounds during the night. She only watched with pleasure as her daughter purchased the shiny, ten-cent watch, at old man Dayton's general store...... and proudly placed it on her wrist.

Carrie, had achieved her goal!

The strong perseverance that Carrie possessed, even as an eight-year-old child, became the sustaining force that accompanied her throughout her life.

For I know the plans I have for you declares the Lord,
to prosper you…
to give you a future and a hope …

Jeremiah 29:11

Chapter Two

As the years went by..... time with family became even more important. The eight children in the Chamberlin family got along very well and Papa Ed's four children, which were the older ones, became models for the younger, Jennings siblings.

Their relatives lived nearby and the Chamberlain family farmhouse was stretched to the limit when they all came to visit. The younger members of the family spilled out onto the porches and the freshly swept, dirt yards. They played games and caught up on the new events in each others life, while enjoying the freshly made syrup candy, which was best when it was still hot enough to wrap around their forks.

The adults filled the small parlor of the farmhouse, sampling the apple or sweet potato pie that Mama Eva and her dear friend, Clara Collier, had made.

The women, passed the time until late into the evening stitching carefully, with love, quilts for their families. Necessary things became social gatherings because time was also a precious commodity.

Stitch a quilt and make a dream, though it was not said verbally, seemed to be the purpose for Eva's many family quilts that she would make and pass down through the generations.

The men-folk, sat on the front porch, considering how they were going to make ends meet on the small profit they made from the crops that year. Even though they did not know how, it always seemed to work out. Oh, they did not have plenty, but they had enough to make it until the next crop.

When the sun began to set, the separate families would get in their wagons and begin their trip home. They drew strength from their time together sharing stories of joys and disappointments. It was good to see family and friends.

The older ladies taught the younger ones to cook, take care of babies and become proficient with crafts that they, in turn, would pass down to their children. They also learned about those homemade remedies, because trips to the doctor or dentist were almost unheard of and made only as a last resort.

Eva's good friend, Clara Collier, was the sister of Ed Chamberlain and the mother of Clint, a handsome youth of sixteen, whose extraordinary attractiveness was not lost on Carrie. She, now fourteen years-of-age, was becoming quite a striking young woman herself. She had dancing brown eyes and skin like buttermilk. She now made her own clothes, having learned her skill from Mama Eva.

Clint's, square jaw and kind eyes melted Carrie's heart each time she saw him. His abundant blondish-brown hair was combed in a becoming *flip,* and his manner was teasing and kind.

The chemistry between Clint and Carrie was undeniable and their shy, stolen glances began to stir in their hearts a love that was to last a lifetime.

Over the next two years Carrie and Clint made a point of being together quite often. He was always the gentleman and she was always the lady. The two of them were not allowed to be alone together because it was not considered "proper" in those days.

They worked and talked together and shared dreams of a future when they would have a family of their own. The peanut shellings, church socials and family times brought new adventure and excitement as Clint and Carrie began to see each other in a new light. Love was on the wing and could not be kept secret.

Although it was not announced and there was no ring on her finger, it was assumed by some and known to Carrie and Clint that they would one day be married.

* * *

The occasional newspaper that reached their farm community, even though a few weeks old, told them of the war that raged in other parts of the world. Radio broadcasts and those occasional newspapers provided sketchy information of world events.

The United States had pulled back from joining in the war. It had not had any impact on the United States as of yet. The leaders of the country had taken a *neutral position,* while a major portion of the world was at war.

Finally, it happened and things began to change. A direct attack on Britain, a major ally, plunged the United States head-long onto the world scene, as a strong force which would not draw back from protecting itself, or its allies.

The war was escalating and young men who were hoping to make a better life for themselves, as well as display their loyalty to their country, enlisted in the armed forces.

Men, young and old, left family and loved ones behind and answered the call to protect the homeland.

Their's was the generation that held the world together for future generations. They became known as the *builder generation*. They all sacrificed and worked hard to ensure

America's freedom as surely as if they were on the battlefields abroad.

Ladies, along with the elderly men filled their places in the factories to help the war effort, while the younger men fought the battles on foreign soil. *Everyone* worked together to make the war effort successful. History would also call them.... the *greatest* generation.

* * *

Clint, who was eager to find his place among the brave young men of America, enlisted in the Army in early July of that year. Immediately, he was sent to the Panama Canal. Carrie and Clint, could not imagine the detour their love was to take.

Carrie, missed him and she was faithful to write Clint every chance she got. He would return those letters with the same love and fervor that she had expressed to him. Their plan was that when his four years of enlistment were over, they would be together again.

World War II was looming however and Hitler was making terrifying progress in his conquest of the world.

Carrie's letters, as well as his mother's letters from home, were the only way of keeping in touch with familiar things and people. Clint looked forward to every one with delight, devouring each word as a tasty morsel.

Jeffery, Carrie's older brother, who was now the image of his father, also wished to show his patriotism and entered the military as a conscientious objector.

Due to his religious convictions he did not want to be involved in conflict, but saw the need to serve his country in some capacity. He was placed in medical facilities and also worked as an airplane mechanic, but he was never required to engage in the battlefield.

For years, Jeffery, had thought of being a minister. Now,

he would have to put that dream on hold. First, he must fulfill his duty to his country. They were at war.

* * *

Carrie, continued to work on the family farm, moving each year as itinerant farmers do, while writing faithfully to Private First Class, Clint Collier.

She and her sisters, Maggie and Hazel, had always enjoyed singing as a past time and they never missed an opportunity to sing at all their family gatherings. The three were encouraged to develop their talent and now, as teenagers, had become very good singers.

Soon they found themselves accepting invitations as they ventured out into the surrounding area of the state. They were becoming well known as event singers. Various church and social groups were always asking the "Jennings Sisters," to be part of their program. The three of them were enjoying the fame they acquired for their *harmonizing*.

Eva's four children did not change their name to Chamberlain, but kept the last name of "Jennings," when their mother married Papa Ed years earlier.

* * *

Every thing was going well as the Chamberlain-Jennings family, settled into their new community for yet another year. Carrie's letters to Clint were filled with exciting details of her life in the community and she kept him informed of what was happening at home. Carrie dropped out of school because she had advanced in age, but not in grades...... due to time lost working on the farm.

She was trying hard to keep the spark alive, but it had been so long since she had seen Clint.

Hazel, with her spunky cuteness, had light brown hair,

dancing green eyes and quick gestures to go with her quick wit. Maggie, had dark-brown hair, an outspoken nature and a firm look, which made the boys even more determined.

Although Carrie was "*spoken for,*" all three girls were becoming young beauties and they were a welcome attraction at any gathering.

* * *

Most families with children, produce at least two who inevitably experience a competition among themselves. The Chamberlains were no different. There had been a teasing rivalry between Maggie and Hazel which had gone on for several years and continued, even though they were now in their early teens. One day, it ended in a decisive encounter.

Carrie, the designated mom in the absence of Mama Eva, was usually around to protect her younger sister, Hazel, from the aggressive Maggie. On one particular day, Carrie was not there to hide Hazel under her protective wing. Hazel, had run as long and as cleverly as she could to avoid Maggie's aggression. Now, she was backed into a corner and had no other choice than to stop Maggie's attack. "If Carrie were here she would help," thought Hazel. "But she is not!"

Hazel's flight, ended in the kitchen. In desperate defense of herself, she quickly picked up the nearest weapon, which was a jagged piece of ice, from a nearby bucket and hurled it with all her might across the room, striking Maggie in the forehead.

Blood spurted profusely through Maggie's cupped hands as she held her wound. Shrieks could be heard for half a mile. Soon afterward, Mama Eva arrived on the scene and the girls received their due punishment. This incident ended the years of pursuit and aggravation that Maggie had waged against her younger sister. Hazel had learned that she *could* protect herself and Maggie, had learned she could not always have her way.

With this decisive event, Carrie realized that she was no longer needed to protect her sister. Hazel, was quite capable of taking care of herself. Maggie did not cause Hazel a problem, ever again. In fact, the rivalry gave way to a close relationship that would last through the years.

* * *

The Chamberlains, like other families, learned that every member has their own personality and qualities that make them the individuals they are.....and you love them anyway. They are part of what makes you who you are and you depend on them for that bond and connection to something that means more than anything else in this world; your family.

The Collier and Chamberlain families taught their children life values, kept food on the table and made their clothes for them.....while teaching them the skill of doing so for themselves.

It was lonely for *all* of them without Clint and Jeffery and hard to imagine how the two of them might feel, so far from home and family for the first time. They missed them greatly and always included them in the prayers said around the supper table each night. They were always in their thoughts and held even more closely in their hearts.

Under the circumstances, living in the great depression with sons away at war, life was "fairly good," at home on the farm.

* * *

"Carrie," Eva called as she was preparing dinner one evening....."go to our new neighbor's house across the field and borrow a cup of sugar. I need it to finish my pie."

Seeing her hesitation, Eva added… "I think her name is Mollie. Just say I asked you to come."

"Oh Mother," Carrie whimpered, "I just came from the garden and I'm all dirty."

"You look fine," prompted Eva.

"Besides…..there is no one there to impress is there?"

"I guess not," whimpered Carrie.

However, even as she spoke, her thoughts flew back a few days to the morning she had seen a young man across the field working. He was strikingly handsome and he had continued looking in her direction for quite some time.

The two had seen each other on occasion, but on that day, he had ventured to speak as he passed close by the fence where Carrie and her sisters were working.

His amazing blue eyes made Carrie quickly catch her breath as they exchanged glances.

"What if *he* were there?"

She did not want him to see her with dirty hands and a torn apron. "I do have some pretty dresses……."

"Hurry"! Eva scolded, breaking into Carrie's thoughts. "I need to get this pie finished for supper."

Seeing that her mother would not be discouraged, Carrie raced into the bedroom which she and her two sisters now shared. Ann and Mary, Carrie's stepsisters, had married and left home last year, leaving more space available.

She took off her apron, threw it toward the bed and stopped on the porch to wash her face and hands. Glancing into the broken mirror hanging from the doorpost, she quickly smoothed her fine-textured blonde hair, tucked her shirt in her overalls and started across the field to borrow a cup of sugar.

Little did she know her life was to take a very sharp detour.

* * *

Oliver Wilkins, was tall and good-looking. He had a strong jaw, clear blue eyes and although he was only twenty-six years old, he had *thinning* blonde hair.

Carrie, walked across the small porch and timidly knocked on the door.

"Hi," Oliver said, with a shyness she did not expect.

"Hello," replied Carrie. Conquering her shyness she said, "Didn't I see you in the field the other day?" Not waiting for him to respond, she quickly continued.....

"I came to borrow some sugar for Mama Eva......if that's okay?"

"Sure," Mollie Wilkins chimed in, having overheard Carrie's request as she entered the parlor.

"How much does she need?" Mollie continued.... making a quick retreat to the kitchen to gather some sugar in a brown paper bag.

"Not much. Just enough for one pie."

Oliver's eyes had not left Carrie since she arrived. Timidly, he began a conversation with her and attempted to walk her out to the gate as she very quickly, but thankfully, accepted the sugar from Mollie's hand and made her way toward home....hardly even stopping to say goodbye.

As Carrie walked, her pace quickened, her heart pounded and her mind became dizzy with excitement. He *was* so-o-o cute, and shy yet. Those blue eyes! It looked as if you could see right through them. She turned to catch a last glimpse of Oliver and found him still watching her as she walked away.

Over the next few days, Oliver came to see Carrie three times. He certainly had serious intentions and it was obvious that Mama Eva and Papa Ed were not happy about that. He was so much older than Carrie was and they hardly knew anything about him.

True, Mollie Wilkins, Oliver's aunt, had told them about a nephew. He had been in the army and was discharged early to return home. He had to help the family when his father lost his hand to cancer. Although family loyalty is an admirable trait, that was *all* they knew about him.

Something about Oliver gave them an uneasy feeling but they could not put their finger on it. Maybe it was the fact that he was just a little *too* interested in Carrie. They felt that she belonged to Clint and this man was moving in while Clint was away.

* * *

New on the scene of Carrie's life, Oliver, was full of dreams and plans for the future and over the next three months, he would talk Carrie into sharing those dreams with him.

Oliver, had worked at the juice plant in Florida during the past winter and came home for the summer to help his family with the crops.

He was convinced that life would be great for the two of them *together* and he would be able to give Carrie the things that she could only dream of if she stayed on the farm.

Carrie's letters to Clint had dwindled to almost nothing, as day-by-day Oliver began to steal her heart. Their relationship escalated quickly and soon Carrie had decided to accept Oliver's marriage proposal.

Carrie, knew her family would object, so she and Oliver made plans to elope.

* * *

Oliver's family, had moved into town from the neighboring farm, just a few weeks before and he was only able to visit Carrie when his uncle Jack would lend him his old car. Since they were not able to see each other as often, they decided to speed up their plans to be married so they could be together *all* the time.

* * *

"You are going to do what?" gasped Hazel, as she raced toward Carrie, taking her sister by the shoulders.

"Don't tell Mama and Papa Ed," whispered Carrie excitedly, as she tried to calm Hazel down.

"Don't tell what?" asked Maggie, as she entered the room.

Carrie, looked thoughtfully at both of her sisters. Finally, she gathered the courage to begin her story.

"Today, when we go to singing school, Oliver is going to pick me up and we are leaving."

Hazel, and Maggie, were astonished at Carrie's statement, but as Mama Eva approached the room.....quietness fell.

"Hurry girls or you will be late for singing school," Eva said, in a cheery, *sing-song* manner.

Carrie's heart was in her throat as she glanced toward her younger sisters, in an effort to survey their intentions. Hazel, seeing Carrie's pleading eyes, looked down and quickly walked out of the room......mumbling something that fortunately was inaudible.

"Yes Mama," Maggie replied, trying to keep things on an even keel. Not because she was happy about the matter, but just because Carrie *was* her sister and they always "stuck together".

After Mama Eva left their small bedroom, Maggie found Hazel and the girls were given assignments to help Carrie finish her plans.

Within minutes, the three of them, quietly and trying not to attract too much attention, made their way from the bedroom out to the splintered, whitewashed porch of their farmhouse and they started down the road to the church.

The *Jennings Trio* studied music each week at their local church and they enjoyed this special time together. However, they all knew *this* day was going to be very different.

Hazel and Maggie, walked along still in stunned silence.

"How could Carrie make such a decision without talking with their mother and how could she disregard the effect it would have on all of them?"

Even though they were the younger of the Jennings sisters, they were well aware of how much their mother would be hurt by Carrie's actions. They did not want their lives changing either and certainly not in such a drastic way.

It was obvious to them that Mama Eva and Papa Ed had their doubts about Oliver Wilkins, and so did they. He was a smooth talker and Carrie had been convinced to leave them, her friends and her whole family. Right then *they* did not like Oliver Wilkins.

* * *

Jeffery, even though away in the army, heard of Carrie's relationship with Oliver and questioned how she could do that to Clint.

Had she forgotten Clint, the handsome young man she was expected to marry when he returned home from the Army?

"How could she toss him aside for Oliver, whom she had known for only three months?"

Marriage! What was Carrie thinking?

The three sisters walked together down the narrow road and they still had not spoken a word when they arrived at the church. Before they entered the little white frame building with its deteriorating steeple and plank porch, they hugged each other tightly.

Silent glances and tear-stained eyes were the only good-bye the three would share before class began.

Carrie, loved her sisters and her family, but right now,

Oliver, was more important in her life.

"Is that the way it is supposed to be?" she wondered.

Carrie, fidgeted uneasily as she opened the worn songbook. Too nervous to sing as she usually did, Carrie glanced over her shoulder, looking toward the door.

The seven notes, creating various tunes, became more distant to Carrie's ears as she became *very* aware of the time.

"Why was Oliver late? Had he changed his mind?"

Imaginary butterflies began to fill Carrie's stomach and it left her feeling queasy. She felt a little lightheaded and she fought for composure as her heart began to pound.

Her sisters, now age twelve and fourteen would be okay, she reasoned. Following the incident with the ice, Carrie realized that Hazel, no longer needed her. She and Maggie had *really* come to love each other.

A few minutes seemed like hours...... until the familiar beep of a car horn was heard from outside. Carrie, sat as if frozen in her seat for a moment, as a tight lump formed in her throat. Her heart began beating more furiously. Gaining composure, she quickly jumped from her seat and started walking down the aisle which led to the church door.

As her hand grasped the door handle, Carrie turned for a last look at her sisters. Hazel's disapproving glance met Carrie's as she turned to walk through the door. Maggie only stared at her in disbelief. Tears stung Carrie's brown eyes, for just an instant, as she slowly walked down the steps and into *her* future.

For better or for worse, Carrie had made her choice. She was marrying Oliver! She would no longer be Carrie Jennings. She would now be Mrs. Oliver Wilkins......whatever that would bring.

* * *

The dusty, country road was bumpy as usual, but the excitement of the moment overcame any discomfort she felt that day. Carrie, laughed and talked with a nervousness that was *unexpected,* even to her.

Oliver's blue eyes looked into hers and her heart melted, as it had so many times over the last three months. He promised her that everything would be fine and she trusted him.

"He is going to be a good husband," Carrie thought, as she settled back into the worn, black leather seat of the old car......and "I am going to be a good wife."

They arrived at the home of the Justice of the Peace late in the afternoon. Carrie, reached for her purse to freshen her powder and realized, that in her haste, she had left it behind in the church. She didn't even have a mirror to look at herself.

Resigned to the fact, that she could not fix what she could not see, she got out of the car to join Oliver. They stepped carefully on the broken, brown, stones which led to the home of the Justice of the Peace.

Oliver, knocked gently on the screen door and hearing an invitation to come in, the two of them entered the parlor seeing an older man hastily arranging his thinning gray hair, as if it was an after thought in getting ready for his guests. He had a quiet manner and a sincere smile.

"So, you want to be married, do you?" he said addressing the couple.

"Yes," replied Oliver.

"Do you have your license?"

"Yes I do," he replied, nervously searching his pockets *twice* before producing the document.

Carrie's heart was racing as never before and if she had not been holding to Oliver's hand, she probably would have fallen in a heap, right then and there.

"Young lady, do you want to marry this man?"

Carrie, was taken off guard.

"Of course I do, that's why I am here."

With a quiet smile, sensing her nervous anticipation, the justice reassured her.

"You only have to answer I do," he said, trying to hold back a smile.

"Oh these are the vows," thought Carrie, her cheeks blushing with embarrassment.

"Young man, do you want to marry this woman.......uh girl?"

"Yes sir I do," replied Oliver, showing confidence.

"Then I pronounce you man and wife. Young man, you may kiss your bride."

"That was it?" Carrie questioned.

Carrie, had dreamed of her wedding day and this was not at all what she had imagined.

As she stood there, in her best pink dress, she pondered the facts in split second intervals. Where were the things she had dreamed of for her wedding day? The fresh white wedding dress, the friends, her family gathered around with smiles and well wishes? Where was the delicious wedding cake, baked by her Mother, Eva? It was to be banana cake, Carrie's favorite.

Carrie's heart sank slightly as she realized that she had decided to forfeit the dreams she had for her wedding day, when she chose to *elope* with Oliver.

Without her permission, a fleeting thought of Clint went through Carrie's mind. "What would *he* think?"

These thoughts quickly vanished however, as Oliver took her in his arms and kissed her. A kiss such as she had not yet experienced, the kiss of a man claiming someone as his own.

Oliver, was ten years older than Carrie and had experienced more of the world.....while Carrie, at sixteen, had not even had a conversation with her mother about the *duties* of a wife. Carrie, had only briefly heard the women talk and only knew a little about what was expected.

Her pulse quicken as she began to think about her wedding night. She felt a *little* afraid. She had enjoyed the delightful sensation of emotions when she and Oliver had kissed but Carrie had not even undressed in the presence of anyone before. At least, not since she was grown.

For the first time, she felt uneasy in Oliver's caress. What would he think of her? Could she please him?

"Uh..hum".... the justice interrupted... "Young man, that will be ten dollars please."

Oliver, handed the Justice ten, crumpled one-dollar bills which he had borrowed from his uncle.

The *ceremony* was over!

Following a hearty handshake and well wishes from the elderly justice, Oliver and Carrie, left to begin their first trip as man and wife. She was now Mrs. Oliver Wilkins. "That has a nice ring to it!" Thought Carrie.

Quickly forgetting her earlier concerns, she and Oliver drove into the night making plans for their new life *together.*

Thy word is a lamp unto my feet
and a light unto my path ......

Psalms 119:105

Chapter Three

It was very late when they arrived at the small, rented room where they would spend their *first* night. As they glanced around, it was obvious that the old, gray, muslin curtains had seen better days and the bed seemed small, even for newly weds.

The old kerosene lamp, sitting on the dresser, produced a dim light which fought to escape the dirty, brown shade which was hanging precariously to one side. The room was stuffy and Oliver raised the window to let in the warm breeze. They were both very tired from the excitement of the day and then the four-hour trip to their destination.

Carrie, had risen early that morning, to take care of stashing the things she would need for her wedding trip. Maggie and Hazel had retrieved them for her later that morning, as planned.

Tired or not.....night had fallen and Oliver was ready to claim Carrie as his own.

Carrie, tried to hide her girlish embarrassment as she slipped slowly into the blue flowered, gingham nightgown which she had been saving. Mama Eva, had given it to her a couple of months before. Of course, Mama Eva did not know she was giving Carrie a gown for her wedding night. It was clean and in good repair, but far from beautiful.

Oliver, had honored Carrie's wish to wait until they were married to express their love. Now, with the formalities over, their wedding night had finally arrived.

He quickly took Carrie in his arms and firmly pressed his lips to hers. Carrie feeling a little nervous, slightly resisted at first, but soon melted into his strong arms as they lay close on the old feather bed.

As the moments passed, Carrie felt emotions she never knew she possessed. Much to her dismay she realized her face was glowing just like the night she, as an eight-year-old child, picked the remaining cotton to reach her goal. This time, she was twice that age and the color of the glow was crimson.

Oliver and Carrie, were joined by love and there, at that moment, they began their journey as man and wife.

The honeymoon was short, as was the money for such a luxury, but the joy they found in each other outweighed the absence of a honeymoon.

* * *

It was time to return home and Carrie's thoughts were of her family. How would Mama Eva and Papa Ed receive them?

Her brother, Jeffery, was sensitive and understanding. What would Clint think when *he* heard of her marriage? Would Hazel and Maggie forgive her? These thoughts plagued her mind.

She was not worried about her stepbrothers and stepsisters because most of *them* had already made the break from the immediate family.

They had married or joined the military and begun their own journey of life, away from the Chamberlain family household.

As they approached Uncle Jack and Aunt Mollie's house, Carrie, was shaking with anticipation. They knew about the wedding because it was Uncle Jack who had loaned Oliver his car. Carrie and Oliver, planned to stay with them until they could get a place of their own.

What about Mama Eva and Papa Ed, did they know yet what had taken place?

Her sisters, Maggie and Hazel, by now would have been forced to tell their mother what had happened the day before. How they had smuggled Carrie's extra clothes out of the barn and Oliver had picked her up at music school in his Uncle Jack's old car.

Her sisters had been none to happy about the event themselves and Carrie knew that her Mother, especially, would not be happy.

Eva, and Clara Collier, were good friends and they had always hoped that Clint, and Carrie would marry.

Eva's feelings about Oliver had not been a secret. She wanted Carrie to take her time, not to be in a hurry and besides, Eva was so fond of Clint. She knew he would be badly hurt by Carrie's actions.

"What had gotten into Carrie anyway?" thought Eva. She was not usually so rash."

Besides, Eva had wanted to *be* at her oldest daughter's wedding.

The hurt Eva felt was still evident as she met Oliver's uncle in town the next week. Days had past and she knew what had happened but she had not seen Carrie.

"Where is my daughter?" Eva demanded....in a somewhat bitter tone.

Jack, being hesitant in answering, received yet another demand from Mama Eva.

"If you don't tell me where she is right now, I am going to get the police to arrest Oliver for taking a minor over the state line," Eva blurted out!

Jack, finally conceded and told her that her daughter was at his house.

"I'll be there shortly," she stated in a calm but firm voice.

Eva was an industrious, hard-working woman, whose strong determination was *passed down* to Carrie. She was also capable of great love and freely distributed it to all her children.

As she wearily made her way to the Wilkin's home, Eva thought back to the young husband she had loved so much and lost and the life she now shared with Ed.

Maybe her daughter had found the love of *her* life. She hoped so, because there was nothing she could do at this point. Maybe her Carrie would be as happy as she had been in the years she was able to spend with Frank, Eva reasoned.

"Love, is what is needed now," she thought, "Not reproach. What's done is done."

Eva, knocked loudly on the door and Mollie Wilkins answered.

"You are here to see Carrie, I imagine."

"Yes I am," said Eva.....trying to keep a civil tone. After all, it was not Mollie's fault. It was Oliver and Jack that had conspired to take her daughter away.

As Eva entered the parlor, Carrie instantly saw the hurt and pain on her mother's face and wished she had done things differently. She quickly invited Eva to the bedroom she and Oliver shared. Without a word, they settled on the feather bed......uneasy in the company of the other for the first time in their life. They sat face to face and Eva broke the silence. "Oh Carrie," Eva said, as she embraced her with a tearful smile. After a few moments of conservation, with all the good will she could muster, Eva accepted Oliver into the family.

"Where will you stay?" asked Mama Eva, managing to hold back her tears.

"Plans have been made to stay here with Oliver's Aunt Mollie and Uncle Jack... just for a while," replied Carrie.

She continued, excitedly telling how they would be saving money to go to Florida so Oliver could again work in the juice packing plant. That should make a good enough living for them. Times were still hard and it was "not going to be easy for them but then again, it was not easy for anyone," she explained.

* * *

Papa Ed, was a serious man not prone to fun and laughter, but he had a light in his eyes that made him approachable and his familiar pipe smelled good as Eva entered the small farmhouse, which they called home.

Ed, remained quiet as usual, while waiting for Eva to begin the conversation. After a thoughtful silence she spoke. "They *are* married.....and at Mollie and Jack Wilkin's house," she said, stopping briefly to stare into space. She began to sift the cornmeal for their supper and added with relief, "At least I know she is okay."

When it came to Eva and her relationship with her children, Ed left her with her thoughts and was just there to comfort and talk, *if* Eva wanted to talk.

Papa Ed, was a steady and dependable man......a hard worker... and he cared for his stepchildren as his own. He had his opinions about child rearing, much the same as Eva's. He was the one who had assigned work chores around the house for all eight children as they were growing up and shared in the discipline. However, he was not one to interfere in the more delicate situations involving Eva's children.

Eva, was a strong woman and only in private did she express the tender feelings she had for her husband, Ed Chamberlain. She had grown to love him for his dedication to her and her children.

A year or so after they were married they had a child of their own, a little girl. She was born prematurely and died shortly after birth. They were both heartbroken, but thankful that they had the opportunity to share the special bond as parents of the same child.....even for a short time. They were very thankful they had been able to raise their two families *together*. They needed each other.

* * *

Clint, learned of Carrie's marriage to Oliver in a letter from his Mother, Clara, a couple of weeks later. He had known something was wrong. Carrie's letters had all but stopped coming and the last couple had been somewhat less expressive than the first ones he had received.

He had *not* guessed that she was interested in some one else. Clint, was definitely heartbroken. His lovely brown-eyed Carrie. How he loved her! What would he do without her in his life?

"Mom," Clint wrote back, "I will always love her." Tears filled Clara's eyes too as she realized that the marriage she and her dear friend, Eva, had always wanted would not take place.

"They were so perfect together. Would Clint ever be happy without her?" Clara wondered.

* * *

September came and Carrie and Oliver had saved enough money to move to Florida.

Two years later...... they would still be struggling.

It was then, that Oliver and Carrie, who was pregnant with their first child, moved back to South Alabama, to work on the farm. They could be close to family there, which was very comforting for Carrie and Oliver tried to find extra work, of any kind, to support his growing family.

Oliver, had saved *some* money from his citrus-packing job and was able to supply their small home with a new bed.... a sofa....a dining room table and a wood burning stove, all for seventy-five dollars.

Among Oliver's many jobs were farming, herding cattle and driving flat bed trucks to transfer supplies from town to town. The supply shortages, which were caused by the war, made transporting goods a pretty decent job in a time when jobs were very scarce.

* * *

The small Alabama town, in which they lived, was a rural farm community and Saturday was the day everyone went to town to do their shopping.

Clara Collier, and Eva Chamberlain had remained good friends. Living close by made it possible for Clara, to stay in close contact with Carrie and know *first-hand* what was happening in her life.

One Saturday, in late August, Clara was in town with Eva and Carrie. She left Carrie, who was now nineteen-years-old and eight months pregnant, to browse at the general store. Soon, Clara returned in a big hurry..... calling out quickly to get Carrie's attention.

"Come here," Clara coaxed gently, as Carrie emerged from the fabric department. "I've got someone I want you to see."

Carrie, followed Clara down the sidewalk, which connected the stores and then around the corner, to where a small group of people was gathered.

Looking toward the group, Carrie's heart jumped! She could not believe her eyes. She was not prepared for *this,* and she turned away, the color draining from her face.

"Could it be him?" she questioned herself.

As she turned and looked again, she realized it was true. Clint was more handsome than ever....especially in his Army uniform. How wonderful he looked to her.

"Come on," insisted Clara, tugging gently on Carrie's hand. The fear and excitement Carrie felt fiercely fought each other, as Clara, ushered Carrie over to see Clint.

Carrie, didn't know if she was going to laugh or cry. "Whatever does he think of me?" she wondered....and it soon became evident that her *fear* was winning the battle.

Soon, she came face to face with Clint. "Hello," muttered Carrie, much like a timid schoolgirl. "Hello Carrie," replied Clint.

His voice was strong and gentle at the same time. It seemed to Carrie as if the disappointment he had felt on learning of her marriage, still resounded in his voice. "How have you been?" he asked.

"Good," said Carrie," knowing full well.... things were not so good in her life right now. She and Oliver had a fight not too long before that and Carrie had gone home to Mama Eva and Papa Ed's for a few weeks. To be honest, she had serious misgivings about her decision to marry Oliver. Nevertheless, those she would keep to herself.

Clint and Carrie, exchanged pleasantries and wished each other well.

She soon made excuses and turned to walk away, stating that she "needed to finish her shopping," but her heart was aching with every step she took.

Clint, stared after her until she was completely out of sight. His heart was heavy and sad beyond words. In the three years since he had seen Carrie, she had made the total transformation from girlhood to womanhood. Carrie, was more beautiful than before but now she belonged to another and very obviously would soon bear his child.

He watched as long as he could and as Carrie turned the distant corner, disappearing from his view, Clint, could not hold back the words as they slipped quietly from his lips.... without his permission.... "Oh Carrie, how I love you. Be well and happy." Tears glistened in his gentle eyes.

* * *

After a few weeks of rest, Clint returned to the army. Soon after, he learned from his mother, Clara, that Carrie had rejoined Oliver and was working on her marriage. They now had a baby boy, which they named after Carrie's father. This crushed all hope that might have been in Clint's heart for a life with Carrie.

Carrie *believed,* as Clint did, that you make a marriage work no matter how impossible the situation seems. At least, they both knew Carrie was going to try.

Clint, with quiet resignation, realized that he must now make a life of his own. In his heart he knew that Carrie would always be special and he would never forget her, even though he himself was to marry a couple of years later.

* * *

Clint, like many of the other soldiers at the army base, frequented a small diner on the main street of a small Georgia town. It was near the military base where he was stationed and the prices were *right.*

On occasion, he had talked with an attractive and friendly waitress, named Millie. One evening, after finishing his meal at the diner, he took the first step and asked her out for dinner. They had a pleasant relationship Clint thought, but nothing serious.

Millie, on the other hand, had been romantically interested in Clint from the time she first saw him. She had quietly decided that she would *work on* getting close to him and their occasional dates became more frequent over the next few months.

One evening, when Millie finished her shift at the diner and Clint had consumed more liquor than he could hold, they left together. No one, other than Clint and Millie ever knew why, or just how, but during the next few days their relationship changed from that of *friends*...... to man and wife.

Clint, was not one to drink and had only partaken of alcohol on very rare occasions in the past. Once, when he was quite young, he and Jeffery, Carrie's brother, took a drink.... "Just to check it out." On another rare occasion, the two of them had gone to town one evening, just to have a "good time." When they returned to the Chamberlain farm, they were very close to being drunk. Of course, it didn't take much to make them "tipsy," because neither had much experience with alcohol.

The fact, that Clint's marriage to Millie took place under such unusual circumstances, proved to be quite a mystery to many people. It was especially troublesome to Clint's family. As far as we know, the couple never offered an explanation.

* * *

A few weeks later....... when Carrie heard of Clint's marriage her heart sank. She knew she had no right to feel that way, but she *had* been thinking more of him lately as her own marriage was deteriorating. In her circumstances, she would not have pursued Clint, but this made everything so final. Now they were *both* married. There was no turning back.

…And now Lord, for what do I wait? My hope is in you…

Psalm 39:7

Chapter Four

Ed and Eva Chamberlain, had farmed other peoples land for many years while they struggled to hold their family together. With sheer determination and God's help, they had been able to survive the depression years and raise their eight children to adulthood. It was time for them to think of other ways they could make a living and perhaps, start a new life in a *new* place.

The last town in north Florida, where they served as itinerant farmers, is where Maggie and Hazel, met and married young military men.

Nick, was a navy man and looked so good to Hazel in his uniform. He was good-natured and he loved to tease.

Maggie's beau, Bill, had also been a sailor and was dark, handsome.....and just what she wanted in a husband.

The couples had met at a dance in town, and the romance began. Both girls were soon married with Mama Eva's restrained approval.

Eva, did not particularly care for the life style Nick had lived as a young sailor and wanted to be sure that he would be willing to settle down and take care of her daughter, Hazel.

The story is told of how Nick came to ask Mama Eva for

Hazel's hand in marriage. He had nervously entered the kitchen one morning, where Eva was making the biscuits for breakfast. He began his speech leading up to the question of marrying her daughter and Mama Eva began to pound the dough, harder and faster, throwing it around in the pan. Nick, grew more nervous as the silent moments went by. Still holding the dough in her hands, as if ready to pitch it in his direction, Eva stated with a determined look on her face........

"If you don't treat her right and can't take care of her......you know where you found her...bring her back!" Nick, was relieved that the moment was over and told Hazel that he was "afraid he was going to be 'wearing' the biscuit dough." The family would laugh about that many times over the years.

Mama Eva did not fool around when it came to her girls!

* * *

Jeffery, by this time, had finished his term in the military and was attending agricultural school.

Eva and Ed, were tired of farming and now with an *empty-nest*, moved to a beautiful town, near the water, in west Florida. They had hopes of being able to *own* some land and maybe even build a home. That would be a *first* for the Chamberlains.

Eva, planned to work as a seamstress and Ed would work as a grounds keeper at the local cemetery. This would sufficiently provide for their financial needs.

Hazel and Maggie, had moved to that same town, with their husbands, a few months before. They told Mama and Papa that this place seemed to hold some promise for a better life. Anything, Eva thought, would be better than the hard farm life they had endured.

Ed and Eva, found an affordable apartment downtown.

Mama Eva with her years of sewing experience was able to set up a custom drapery business, working from her home and Papa Ed worked at the cemetery.

Later……the two would purchase a piece of land and build a small two-bedroom home where they would live for the rest of their days. It would not only provide shelter for them, but it would house any of Eva's children or grandchildren as well. All were welcome at Mama Eva and Papa Ed's, especially family.

* * *

Florida proved to be very different. The Chamberlains had exchanged the red clay and sandy loam of Alabama…..for soft, white sand and sometimes just plain, black dirt .

Maggie and Hazel, lived close by which made it nice for Eva, but she prayed constantly for Carrie who was still in the back woods of Alabama. She knew how hard farm work could be and as a mother she wished that her daughter did not have to experience the same life that had aged her well beyond her years.

* * *

Foster, was now a cute, blonde, two-year-old with brown eyes like Carrie's. Darla Kay, their second child, had just been born. Carrie, now had two children to care for…… living in a remote area, with her husband pursuing any available job to provide for his family.

The house they lived in was humble, to say the least, but Carrie did not mind that. What she did mind, was that it was so far in the back woods. It was surrounded by overshadowing trees and sounds, that took on an ominous feeling as the sun set……the darkness fell…..and Oliver was not yet home.

Fear and loneliness, were the emotions that Carrie found dominating her life. Oliver, had started drinking, just enough to "keep warm," out in the cold and "keep him awake," on long road trips.

He was later than usual coming home one night and Carrie began to worry that something had happened to him.

Later that evening, as she looked out the front door in anticipation, she saw a man in the distance leading a horse, with another man barely able to stay on the horse's back. As they were approaching, she realized it was Oliver's dad leading the horse with Oliver, swaying unsteadily and haphazardly across the horse's back. A few minutes later, they arrived at the front yard gate.

"Sorry honey," Oliver said with a slur, sliding from the horse's back and falling to the ground in front of her feet.

"I'm as drunk as a skunk," Oliver said....looking up with a silly smile. He had never been drunk before and his surprising mannerisms brought a smile to Carrie's face. She was relieved that he was home and okay.

* * *

What Carrie thought to be a one-time event began to happen repeatedly. Before long, Oliver, had made a *habit* of drinking. Whether it was to keep warm, or to take the edge off his own discouragement in that hard time we do not know. Nevertheless, it became a very frequent occasion when he would come home in a drunken stupor, providing no companionship or support for Carrie, who found herself *alone* most of the time.

The next few months became long and lonely for Carrie. She had to leave the children alone in the small back-woods home, as she chopped wood for the stove or worked in the nearby field trying to provide food for her table.

* * *

Foster, now four, was cute as a button, with pleading brown eyes but he was having problems walking and talking normally. Carrie, worried that the fall he had taken from a high bed, when just a few months old, had somehow caused his developmental problems. She left him with pillows stacked around to secure him, but he had worked his way to the edge and fallen between the unfinished wall and the bed, striking his nose and head on the iron bed frame. Against Carrie's wishes, Oliver decided that Foster did not need to see the doctor, even though his head, face and nose were badly bruised and swollen. Carrie, would always wonder if they had done the right thing.

* * *

Darla, with her blue eyes and curly blonde hair, was now two-years-old. She was at an adventurous age and wanted to investigate everything. Carrie, constantly worried about her young children while she was working outside, away from the house, but chores and garden work could not be accomplished with children around your feet.

There were no modern playpens and child restraints available then. Quite the reverse, there were many dangers that you could only pray your children would avoid. The deep well, from which they drew their water....the fire in the fireplace, which kept them warm.... or the hot pot-belly stove, where she cooked their meals, just to name a few.

Foster, at age four was given the task of "looking out" for his sister. In fact on one of those days, when he was in charge, he was trying to help Darla and he cut her hand very badly with a butcher knife. Because of his developmental problems Foster could not run fast and his little legs were *racing* as he ran toward the field. He was making slow progress because his motion was more up and down than forward. However, he ran as fast as *he* could searching for his mother, crying loudly,

"I cut tister's hand! I cut tister's hand!"

Carrie, finally hearing Foster's tearful cries, ran as fast as she could, leaving him behind in the field. She found Darla in a puddle of blood, sitting on the back porch with her hand bleeding profusely. Blood was running through the wooden slat floor and onto the ground below. Through all the blood, Carrie could see that the thumb was barely attached to the rest of Darla's hand.

She wrapped the wounded hand with the first cloth she could find and grabbing Darla up in her arms, she ran for the dirt road near their house where she hoped to find *someone* to take her to a doctor in town.

Usually, she could see her neighbor working in his field, but not today. With no one in sight, she took Darla in one arm and dragging Foster with the other, she walked as quickly as she could toward the neighbor's house a mile away.

"Help me, help me," Carrie called, as she saw a man in the distance.

Her neighbor, seeing the situation, gathered them into his old car and drove as quickly as he could into town.The cloth bound around Darla's hand was soaked with her blood and Carrie worried that they would not be able to save her thumb.

"Oh God," she whispered softly, "please let my baby's hand be okay."

She felt a little guilty for not being in the house to take care of her children. But she also knew she had no choice.

The doctor stitched the hanging, bloody thumb back into place and they hoped for the best. Fortunately, it healed well and in a few weeks it looked like everything would be normal, leaving only a large scar on Darla's tiny hand.

"What would have happened if Mr. Tucker had not been home?" Carrie worried.

"What am I doing in this God-forsaken place?" She had never been more miserable. Something *had* to change!

Over the next few months Carrie suffered from malaria, an enlarged liver and other physical problems. She had come to the end of herself. She could no longer ignore *her* unhappiness and her physical well being, to say nothing of that of her children. She found herself greatly depressed and sinking into despair.

* * *

One evening, while she and the children were alone, the latch on the back-porch door began to shake back and forth. The lock was held together only by an old fence wire, which Carrie had wrapped repeatedly around the broken lock, to secure it.

She quickly took a large knife from the drawer and crouched near the kitchen door. Darla and Foster, were playing contentedly in the front room. She held the knife close to her chest and *prayed* that the man would leave. Her heart was pounding. After what seemed an eternity, the rattling stopped and Carrie heard footsteps retreating across the porch and soon...... there was silence.

Jumping up, Carrie grabbed her children and ran for Oliver's parents house just up the dirt road. After that, she stayed with his parents until he came home each evening.

A little more time passed and when Oliver came home *late* one evening she had come to the end of her rope. She felt no restraint in telling him firmly,

"I can't stay here any longer on the back side of nowhere, wondering if you are coming home each night. I have had it and something has to change!"

The farm was a dream of Oliver's and he had hoped it would make a living for them, along with his truck driving job.

Carrie, felt bad that it had not worked out, but she could no longer deal with the sickness, loneliness and sheer desperation that she felt.

Oliver, had taken out insurance on the farm a few months before so an idea sparked in his mind. When the house mysteriously burned one night, while Carrie was visiting her in-laws, she knew better than to ask questions. She was so desperate that she didn't care. She was just glad they were finally going to move back to town.

When people wondered about the cause of the fire, Carrie didn't say a word and never told anyone of what she knew to be a fact. Oliver, had burned the house.

* * *

Months later, Oliver and Carrie were having even more problems and she felt it would be best if she left and found a place near her mother and Papa Ed in Florida. Surely, they would let her and the children stay until Carrie could find work and get a place of her own.

She couldn't tell them all the reasons she was leaving. The fire....the time Oliver spent hiding from the law, in a town one-hundred miles away, while she worked in the sewing factory to keep food on the table for the children.

The cattle that Oliver and his brother had stolen, from a stockyard in Florida, landed his brother in jail. But Oliver, hid from the authorities and wrote letters home to Carrie to let her know where he was. He was in hiding for several months.

Carrie, needed and wanted something better for herself and her children and she purposed to try.

* * *

Clint, hoped to leave the army when his four-year enlistment period was over but his request was denied. The army needed every available man they had and would call up many more in the days to come.

The Japanese, had bombed Pearl Harbor on that terrible day in December of 1941, and the United States was drawn even deeper into the war. They attacked us on our own soil and now our country was involved, whether they wanted to be or not. They had no choice.

In 1942, Clint's division was *called up* to join thousands of other soldiers, already in the heat of battle, as the war intensified in Germany, France and other regions of the world. World War II was well underway.

* * *

"Hold that line," shouted Sergeant Browning, as Clint, and the other foot soldiers hit the ground running. His platoon was dumped from the back of a truck near a trail leading into some distant trees. Clint, had not yet seen battle but the artillery in the distance brought a terrible reality to the moment.

The battle was underway and his unit had been called in as reinforcements to a platoon, which was being overrun at the front line. Many men had been killed already and their bodies were strewn along the path as the new forces advanced toward the front to engage the enemy. The fight was vicious, with more ground being lost than taken.

The tired troops fought valiantly, but after many days of enemy sniping from the trees and trenches.....and often hand-to-hand combat, Clint and the few remaining soldiers, were taken prisoner by the Germans.

Clint, endured nine months in a primitive prison camp in Germany, where he, along with his fellow soldiers, were brutalized on a daily basis and hungry and thirsty most of the time.

Many times, the dew on the fence was the only source of water and the food was often filled with maggots. During the months and for some of them years, memories became permanently etched in the minds of the occupants in that camp. Things that they would wish to forget......but would haunt them for the rest of their lives. At that point, it was questionable how long that would be.

Only journalists and historians wish to write about and report on such events. Those who experience combat and war of any kind *always* pray to forget.

Clint's days in the prison camp were long and void of human joy. Not only was the food disgusting, but the beds were nothing more than a piece of cloth placed over *your* space on the cold ground.

Clint's thoughts, very often, were of his family and friends back home.

Millie, was on his mind many times.......but with the memory of Carrie still fresh, the image of her face appeared before him during the long lonely nights. Whether it was a dream or a true vision he could not tell. Reality and hope blurred together.

Thoughts of home, a warm bed and times *past* with family and friends proved to be the escape that he needed to survive under these unspeakable circumstances.

* * *

Clint, was one of the highest-ranking soldiers at the prison camp. Because of this, he became the spokesperson for the the American soldiers held there. He was put in charge of the detail to bury men who died during the night from the starvation, the cold, or the disease for which they received very little medical attention.

One day, Clint on behalf of his men, had been summoned to a meeting in the make-shift office of the German General, when he heard a disturbance outside.

"Listen!" shouted one of the prisoners, as he ran toward

the tall barbed-wire fence in the compound. Several others began hobbling along, as best they could, with their makeshift splints and injuries. Some had lost limbs and others eyes……while some were too thin and weak, from lack of food, to keep up.

"Artillery in the distance," he continued.

Clint, ran out to see a German soldier running past him, shouting alternately in English and German …….

"Everyman to his post, we are under attack!"

He quickly joined the rush of prisoners to see the Russian army bearing down on the camp. The approaching soldiers greatly outnumbered those on duty there. It didn't take them long to overrun the camp and free the American soldiers and the other prisoners. For some it had been years and for Clint, nine long months of imprisonment.

The feeling was indescribable as Clint, along with many others, was set free. Their emotions were truly overwhelming as tears of joy ran down their faces. Cheers, even from that malnourished group, resounded through the air with gusto. Smiles, which had long been absent, returned to their faces.

Although this had not been the Russian armies main assignment on that day, the men who were freed from prison didn't care who did it, or how. They were free and on their way home. They were *truly* thankful!

* * *

The liberated troops were sent home for a little rest and Clint, as well, returned to his home in Alabama. He spent time with his family and loved ones trying to forget the horrible memories of war that weighed heavy on his mind.

Of course, Carrie was at some of these gatherings because she, also, was family by marriage.

With Millie by Clint's side and Carrie with Foster and

Darla, now ages three and five, she and Clint could see only a small glimmer of the love they once shared.

Carrie's life with Oliver on the backside of nowhere....and now in a small house in town, mixed with the new revelation of Oliver's character brought her respect for him to a new low. Things were rocky to say the least. She had definitely decided that it would be best if she started over again. And this time, without Oliver!

In the spring, Carrie and the children said goodbye to Oliver....climbed on a greyhound bus.....and with determination left to begin a new life.

* * *

Clint, for various reasons, had decided to stay in the military and make it his career. There was nothing but farming if he came home and he had "taken a liking" to the regimented discipline and stability of military life. He also liked the travel it could afford he and Millie. They enjoyed seeing other parts of the world as a military family and as he left to return overseas, it seemed his life was set.

Carrie, was nowhere in the picture.

Now to Him who is able to do exceedingly, abundantly, above all we are able to ask or think according to the power that works in us……

Eph 3:20

Chapter Five

Over the next few months.....Oliver, struggled to find work. He was also beginning to realize that he missed Carrie and the children and during the quiet, lonely nights, he remembered Carrie's words,

"If you can really quit drinking and be a husband and father there may be hope for us. Otherwise, I am gone for good."

Oliver, *wanted* to quit drinking, but could he? It seemed as if alcohol had become a constant and comfortable companion to him over the last few years. He really didn't know if he *could* give it up, but he did want to try.

"I love Carrie more," he thought, and he loved his children. Oliver, hung on to the questionable hope in Carrie's last words to him as they played over in his mind......"If you can stop drinking and really be a husband we have a chance."

One morning, Oliver rolled out of bed, shaved, dressed in his best clothes and looked into the mirror. He saw a man who was desperately lonely and going nowhere. With determination, he climbed into his *old* model, black pick-up truck, which had seen better days and left his home in Alabama. He was on his way to Florida!

As he drove down the country roads, with the dust flying behind him, he purposed something in his heart. He would win her back! He could and would convince Carrie to give him a *second chance*.

* * *

Carrie's ability as a seamstress, which she learned at the knee of Mama Eva, helped her to make a home of the small, but adequate, house trailer that sat in Mama Eva's and Papa Ed's back yard.

The weather was hot in July and the small trailer provided shade from the sun, but at the same time the tiny, porthole windows blocked out the summer breeze. The trailer was white, originally, but the rust was now creeping over the top and slowly making its way down the side, giving it a dirty look.

As Carrie worked, the perspiration gathered on her forehead in glistening beads and began to run down her face. She did her cleaning on Saturday, because her weekdays were filled with working at the awning factory where she was a seamstress. Then, coming home.....already tired....to care for her children.

Wiping her face, with her faded flour sack apron, she began to prepare the evening meal which consisted of dry lima beans and cornbread.

Carrie's mind was filled with plans for her small family and dreams of a better life for herself. She could not deny, however, the emptiness she felt on the inside. She was so deep in thought that she almost did not hear the timid knock on the screen door.

"Oh...Who could that be," she thought?

She was not in the mood to talk with anyone now and she certainly didn't want to be seen, given her present condition.

Carrie, began walking slowly toward the door. She did not

have many visitors. "Maybe it is Mama Eva," she thought.

As she came nearer to the door....she saw him standing there.

"Oliver," Carrie gasped with surprise, as she carefully opened the door.

"What are you *doing* here?"

She instinctively smoothed the fine, blonde hair from her forehead and quickly adjusted her apron.

She was surprised to see him. Some part of her was excited, while the other part was afraid of exactly what Oliver had come there to do, win her back.

Oliver, shifted his position uneasily as he answered, "I came to see you."

"I miss you and the kids and I want to talk with you. Can I come in?"

Carrie, knew in her mind that Oliver had not made great changes. However, after talking with him for over an hour, she could see that he *wanted* to change and he promised once again that he would.

She looked into his clear, blue eyes and remembered the tender feelings that had brought them together...... and times *had* been hard without him. Maybe, just maybe, they could make it this time.

"Okay," Carrie whispered, as Oliver embraced her tenderly........

"We can do this if we work together. Promise me that you will value our marriage and you will work *hard* on stopping your drinking."

"I promise," said Oliver, as he held her close.

A tender kiss sealed the promise and within just a few days they moved into a duplex apartment, several blocks from the awning factory where Carrie worked.

* * *

Oliver, began right away, looking for work and found a job at a lumber company near by, which was also involved in construction. Oliver and Carrie, began saving for a "new future," together.

They had their eye on a lot, on the other side of town, which was large enough to build a home for themselves and then another for a rental property.

When they had saved enough money, Oliver had also gained sufficient construction experience, at his job, to do some of the work on the house himself. Now, they would be able to build their first, *new* home.

The children were growing daily it seemed and at the ages of six and eight, they would have the yard space they needed to play. As an added bonus for Carrie, there was a church just down the street. They were also able to buy a used car.

"Things are going quite well," thought Carrie. With Hazel and Maggie also living in town, they were able to visit and encourage each other. Foster and Darla, were now settled in school and they were on their way to their new life.

Mama Eva, and Papa Ed, were none to happy with the chain of events, because they did not think Oliver would, or could change. They feared that Carrie would find herself disappointed ....once again.

* * *

Carrie's brother and sisters were doing well, with families of their own. Jeffery, had begun to attend Bible College, studying to become a minister. He had put this desire on hold, earlier in his life, in order to serve his country and now God was giving him a second *chance* to fulfill his dream. His sensitive and quiet nature made him perfect, for what he considered a *calling* to the ministry.

At college, Jeffery met Emma, a wonderful young woman with long blond hair and so soft-spoken, you really had to concentrate to hear her words.

She was in sharp contrast to Carrie and her sisters. Hazel, could talk the socks off anyone and Maggie, made herself known, with no questions asked. Carrie, was the more quiet, inward girl in the family but strong enough speak up, if necessary, to protect herself or her children.

Emma, also had a call to ministry and she would be the perfect mate for Jeffery. He knew Emma was the one for him, after only a short time and he finally found the nerve to *pop* the question. The two were married right after their graduation from Bible College and began their ministry in a small church in south Florida.

* * *

Carrie, continued working hard. Besides caring for her family, her time was spent cooking, cleaning and working a shift at the awning factory in town. She and Oliver were busy and did not realize that their children were experiencing difficulties in coping with the constant changes in their life.

Darla, was affected emotionally by the unsettled nature of her parent's relationship and her insecurity would last a long time. She also had problems that were *hidden* to Carrie and Oliver.

Darla, depended on daydreams to keep her life calm and as a means of playing......due to the lack of toys or gadgets. On one occasion, her feelings erupted in very noticeable way. Darla, received a new coat, which was a rare thing. One day, while she was at school, she cut her beautiful, blue, coat in shreds...... for no obvious reason. Neither the teacher, nor her mother, understood her actions and Darla was too young to understand why she had done such a thing. She cried and asked her mother to forgive her, but she still had no answer as to why she had shredded her coat.

Darla, was great at the game "let's pretend," because she

could make her life whatever she wanted by pretending.

Around the age of nine or ten, she began to have a continuing dream of violence against her. Night after night......this same dream would awaken her in fear.

A man with a large knife was always chasing her trying to kill her. As she crouched, hiding behind a dresser, he would find her and would raise the knife to start stabbing her. Darla would wake up with her heart pounding and so scared that she could not even call for her mother. This was to plague her for several years.

Foster's actions also demonstrated that he had not been spared the problems between his mother and father. He was unsure of himself and felt he was less loved than his sister was. Nothing he did was *right*.....and he was a disappointment to his father. Foster, did not have the *strong man* temperament that Oliver had wanted in a son.

Oliver, did not understand anything about expressing love and giving motivation. He only added to Foster and Darla's feelings of inferiority, by his taunting that they "were no good," and "would never amount to anything."

Foster, was more pliable and sensitive and took to heart the things planted in his mind....... believing what his father had said.

Darla, although very sensitive, was more determined by nature. Seemingly, she refused to let it get her down. This proved to be an outward-shell, because she was debilitated by her own feelings of inferiority for many years.

Oliver and Carrie, were working on their marriage and struggling to make *ends meet*. They had little time to recognize what their children were experiencing, let alone why.

* * *

Finally, their new house was completed and Carrie and Oliver, moved their family into the two-bedroom, gray and white, shingled home...... on the other side of town. Though the house was small, it was adequate. Foster, now age twelve and Darla, age ten shared a room.

The family enjoyed the large front lawn, which was long and expansive. Colorful wild flowers grew at certain times of the year, providing a pleasant setting for Carrie and the children. Oliver, did not notice such things, or if he did never made mention of it.

The near by trees were great for climbing and Darla found her *first* best friend, Patty, who lived on the next street. She and Foster also had a boxer dog named "Pluto." He was a good dog and provided a companionship that they both needed.

Money was scarce, but Carrie and Oliver were working hard to provide for their family. Birthdays and Christmas passed with little mention, for a couple of years.

It was in this difficult time that Darla wrote her first song, beginning to show her talent for music. She was proud of her accomplishment, "I'm Getting Nothing for Christmas," until she saw the hurt look on her mother's face when she learned of it.

* * *

Oliver, soon found that his daily struggle, was made easier with his companion of the past.....and again he became a frequent drinker. This time, he was abusive verbally *and* physically. He was an unwelcome sight for his family. Foster and Darla, always dreaded the time he would come home, because they knew he would be drinking and would cause problems.

Carrie, discouraged by Oliver's actions, often remembered the days she had enjoyed going to church with Mama Eva and her brother and sisters and how they enjoyed their faith together.

She thought of her sisters, Maggie and Hazel, and the good times they shared as they sang the songs of the church for their community. It had been years since she had thought about those days.

"My, it seems like such a long time ago," she thought.

She missed her life..... as it was before and with Oliver's drinking increasing, along with the knowledge of his recent infidelity fresh in her heart, she turned to prayer once again.

Carrie, arranged for Foster and Darla to attend the little church in their new neighborhood. They had a new home and now it was time to start a new habit for her *children* although her own faith seemed but a glimmer of the past.

"God, I can't pretend to serve you and until I can serve you with all my heart, I will not give the impression that things are okay," Carrie prayed.

"Please God, keep my children in *your* care."

With Foster and Darla approaching the teen years Carrie, was a little surprised when she realized she was going to have another child. The thought brought mixed feelings. The timing certainly wasn't the best.

Oliver, was still working in the building business and Carrie, was taking care of their new home and their growing family. She had to leave her job and they only depended on Oliver's income to provide for their needs.

Things grew worse and more frequently in the evenings, Oliver would come home drunk and life began to be unbearable for Carrie.

No one, liked to see him come home. "Carrie! Get me something to eat," yelled Oliver, as he entered the door each evening, usually in a drunken stupor. He was always late getting home and she and the children had come to realize what that meant. Darla and Foster, would find something to do in their small, shared bedroom unless they were not able to get out of his sight soon enough. Then, their father would gave them a task to accomplish.

Most of the time, Darla's nightly task was to take off her father's shoes and clean his dirty feet and toenails. He would taunt her as she worked, making silly drunken remarks and Darla could feel the resentment rise from deep inside.

Oliver, was silly, until he became angry.....which didn't take long. Each evening, as soon as they finished their work, Darla and Foster would leave the room. At times, trouble would start at the supper table and Darla, would grab Loren, who was just a baby, and run with him to the bedroom to protect him, she thought, from her father. She sat on her bed holding him close and waiting to hear what would happen next.

Even if they were not in the same room, she and Foster could still hear what was going on and they were afraid for themselves and their mother as the conversation grew loud and hostile.

Oliver, could become violent when drinking and he had struck Carrie more than once. Carrie, did attempt to take care of herself but sometimes it was futile. She always did her best to meet his demands, but whatever she did was not good enough for Oliver and this made a very unhappy situation for her and the children.

"How could things have turned out this way?" Carrie sobbed privately. She didn't want the children to see.

"What happened to the man that I married, with the beautiful, blue eyes that could melt my heart?"

"God, please give me strength to raise my children properly."

Carrie, continued to sob as she prayed and she knew that in order to keep her sanity she would have to, once again, ask Mama Eva if she could stay with her and Papa Ed.

* * *

After she and the children moved out, Oliver found times to meet with the children and ask them to *beg* their mother to "come back to him." Putting the children between them, was one of Oliver's ploys to win Carrie back. Sometimes, it was convincing and sometimes not.

Darla and Foster, certainly did not like being used as a tool by their father, against their mother, but they had no choice. They would, at Oliver's prompting, ask her to go back to live with him, while hoping desperately that she would say no. They did not enjoy the disputes between their parents, whether together or apart. After all, they were only children and being responsible for their parent's relationship was too large a task for them.

* * *

Clint and Millie, were traveling the world at this time, living in exotic places like Japan, Germany and any place his military assignments required them to live.

They were enjoying a good life and had learned to love each other, but still had no children. Clint, had sustained an injury during the war which they believed made him unable to have children. He stepped on a mine while scouting out an area for the advance of the infantry against enemy territory. His foot, leg and groin area were seriously injured. The wound healed well but they did not know the extent of the damage for a long time.

Millie's two children, from her previous marriage, were still kept secret from Clint's family, as well as Clint and Millie's closest friends and neighbors. Millie, was divorced when she met Clint, in the decade of the forties. It was rare that women took such a step, even in dire circumstances, at that time in history. Divorce, was not an acceptable solution and was not *thought well of* in society, especially not southern-society. Millie, was afraid Clint's family would not understand. After all, the unusual circumstance of their marriage was enough to contend with, as far as Clint's family was concerned. They found out about his marriage, after the fact, and it was not accepted in a favorable manner.

Millie, decided before she met Clint, that the children would be better off with her mother and left them in her care. Clint, always honored her wish to keep her children a secret and never spoke of it to anyone.

* * *

As a part of the military, they spent much of their life away from *home* and family and only in later years, were Clint and Millie able to settle down in their small home in Georgia.

Clint, trained young recruits at the same military base where he and Millie had met. They purchased a home, while on furlough a few years before and now, after returning, life was good for them.

Clint, became known as "the preacher," because of his public display of faith. The term was not used in a derogatory manner, but rather as a term of respect. As a Sergeant Major, he earned the favor of those around him and he became known as *a fair, but firm* man in the military arena. Clint, was active in his church and was always willing to lend a helping hand, wherever he could and always with joy.

As the years went by, Clint would occasionally think of his lost love.

"Carrie, how are you today," he would think, as he went about his daily tasks. He always wondered what could have been and hoped that she was well and happy. However, the last he had heard......that was not the case.

* * *

Shortly after their third child, Loren, was born, Oliver, convinced Carrie once again that he could change......that they could still make a life together.

They had just been through one of Oliver's *girlfriend* episodes and he had even brought this one to the house. Darla and Foster, couldn't help but notice and felt uneasy when she was there. Oliver and Carrie, had weathered this storm and now they were moving on with their life.

Dutifully, she packed up her belongings, disrupted her children's lives and moved to North Florida to follow yet another of Oliver's dreams......a restaurant.

The small town was growing quickly and held promise for new businesses. They rented a two-bedroom home near the high school. And down town, on Main Street, they opened a *family-style* restaurant. Oliver, had *really* hoped to open a bar but the city regulations would not allow a bar in that location.

Foster and Darla, soon enrolled in Jr. High and began a new phase of their lives. Darla's gymnastic ability won her a spot on the cheerleading team and Foster struggled, as usual, to make friends and be a *part* of the group. Darla, even though she was very shy and inward, was discovering some of her abilities in the area of athletics and singing.

She became the star of the Jr. High "sock-hops" and was having a somewhat good time for the *first* time in her life.

Carrie, saw her daughter begin to blossom as a young woman and Darla had her first boy friendship when she was twelve. Carrie, made a beautiful dress of blue taffeta with netting and sequins, for Darla to wear to a special dance. The dress would also double as a gown, for Darla's first and only singing recital. She had taken singing lessons for a few weeks, but had to quit..... because they could not afford the expense.

When Darla saw the dress, she thought her mother had done the miraculous. From the time she was little she loved pretty dresses. At the age of two or three, Darla would rub them and say they were "pitty." This time was no different. The dress was beautiful and Darla felt very special.

* * *

Foster, suffered from the continued taunting he received from Oliver. He and Darla, were told that they were not as *good* as other people were and they were incapable of accomplishing anything. This naturally had a negative impact on Foster.....because he still *believed* what he was told by his father. Darla, resisted the idea.

Carrie, was a stay-at-home mom during this time and spent her days caring for Loren, Foster, and Darla, while Oliver was working hard on the restaurant.

It did not take long for things to change, yet again. The promises, though truly meant, when they were made, soon gave way to Oliver's old nature.

Late nights and infidelities on Oliver's part brought fresh heartache to Carrie and the children as well. Although they didn't know specifics, they *knew* and could feel that things were not good. They saw the result in their home.

* * *

During this time, Darla was invited to attend a small church in their community. She found great interest in the *family* feeling of the people there and she was invited to sing with the small choir. Foster attended sometimes, but Darla was the most interested. She was becoming aware of spiritual things for the first time.

She had encouragment in that direction during an incident that happened at, of all places, her home. Just a short time before, she had seen her father receive a miracle from God and in her estimation, he did not *deserve* it.

Darla, was puzzled, then amazed, when she saw her father bow his head for prayer when the TV preacher prayed for those with afflictions. As the preacher prayed with enthusiasm, Darla, watched her father intently. At the conclusion of the prayer, Oliver immediately jumped up from the chair where he was sitting, removed the sling and ran to the kitchen to embrace Carrie.....waving his arm, demonstrating his healing.

A couple of days earlier, after being out all night, Oliver entered the living room of their home with dried blood on his clothes. His arm, was injured so badly he could not use it.

In his drunkenness, while driving home in the wee hours of the morning, he had *flipped* his truck. His head had some cuts and bruises, but his arm was severely injured. His doctor had ordered him not to work and to keep his arm in a sling for a few days. He could not lift it on his own.

Darla, couldn't get the image out of her mind. "How could God do such a thing for him?" she thought.

"God, must be very loving and forgiving."

Even in Darla's bewilderment, it was good to see a look of happiness return to her mother's face, as she embraced her father. Carrie, smiled for the first time in a long time and shed tears of joy at Oliver's demonstration of faith.

* * *

The family soon moved to a small trailer on the outskirts of town, with plans to build another new house. There was barely enough room to turn around in the trailer home. It was approximately ten-feet wide and twenty-five feet long. It had a combination kitchen-living room, a very small airplane size bath, a small berth-type bed, off the hall and a cramped, little bedroom with a built-in dresser and double bed for Oliver and Carrie. Darla, now thirteen, slept on the small berth bed and Foster slept on the fold-out sofa in the living room each night. Loren, slept beside Foster on a *small floor pallet.*

Carrie, was determined to make the best of it and soon adjusted, making her children as comfortable as she could.

Carrie, was quite the artist with hair styling and soon became popular with "finger waving" the neighbor girls hair. Darla, was now becoming a young woman and she enjoyed the benefits of her mother's hair styling talents as well.

Foster, as you might guess, was still struggling with his inferior feelings which made him unable to attract friends.

Loren, now three, blonde and beautiful was Oliver's very favorite child. He was so proud of Loren and thought that he could do no wrong. Oliver, *finally* had the son he always wanted. However, Oliver was still making life uncomfortable for Carrie, and the children, by his drinking and the lifestyle that it brought.

* * *

On a summer evening, around eight o'clock, Carrie had finished her ironing, in her outside utility room. She had just returned to the trailer, when a car pulled up outside their home. A man.... dirty, scruffy and unknown to Carrie, appeared at the opened screen door. As he took a deep breath, to ask his question, the pungent smell of alcohol filled the air.

"Oliver at home?" he asked..... with a slur to his speech.

"Y-e-s," she replied hesitantly, as Oliver came toward the door.

"Who wants to know?" asked Oliver, stepping closer.

He could see the old, beat up car parked outside and he recognized the man in the car as someone he had a problem with, a few days before, at the restaurant. It had not been pleasant and the two had parted with bad feelings and promises that it was *not* the end of the matter.

Oliver, could see the cold metal of the shotgun the man was holding, as it glistened in the moonlight. A feeling of fear rose in him and he quickly made a dash for the back door. He struggled to squeeze himself out of the small door and began a labored run for the neighbor's house across the street. The extra weight Oliver carried, because of his age and his drinking, slowed him down quite a bit.

Carrie, stepped outside, just as the second man jumped from the car and hurried toward her, with his gun outstretched.

In the moonlight, he saw someone crossing the street and he turned the gun and took aim for Oliver, as he ran.

"Don't shoot!" cried Carrie.....struggling to push the gun upward.

"That is my child running across there!"

The man pulled away and readjusted his aim, but it was too late. Carrie's actions had bought Oliver the time he needed to get to the neighbor's house, where he asked for a gun. Thankfully, the neighbor refused.

Carrie, cried excitedly again to the men, "Get away from here, or I'll call the police."

Luckily, the man with the gun returned to the car and they drove away.....swearing loudly.....*promising* they would be back.

Carrie, stood there trembling and her heart sank with fear at her own actions. What she did had been instinctive and foolish, but it had also saved Oliver's life.

"Could it get any worse?" Carrie wondered.....as tears filled her eyes and spilled onto her face, still white with fear. She wiped away her tears, with hands still shaking and returned inside to reassure her children, even though she herself was badly shaken.

Her anger with Oliver, for bringing that kind of situation into their home, simmered below the surface like a strong volcano ready to erupt. She was just waiting for the proper outlet.

* * *

The new house, with its three small bedrooms, was completed a few weeks later and the Wilkins family moved in. The newness of the house brought a wave of hope for a clean start.

They bought new white provincial furniture for Darla and Carrie sewed curtains for the windows. Foster, got new furniture and both he and Darla had a room of their own for the very *first* time.

Darla, was so happy and excited. On the other hand, she felt the unhappiness that was evident in their home and in her heart. Even now, she would escape through the world of make believe. Reality would soon take the place of fantasy as Darla grew in age and understanding.

With the new house and the expenses it brought, it became necessary for Carrie to work outside the home once again. Darla and Foster, now age thirteen and fifteen, had many tasks to perform before and after school each day. Laundry, dishes, making beds and caring for Loren was a normal day for Darla. The north Florida mornings were frigid as she hung out the laundry before leaving for school. The clothes were frozen stiff by the time she took them down, at the end of the school day, to sprinkle them for ironing.

Foster, was also given assignments, but when he did not complete them, he was derided by Oliver as a "no good" child.

Carrie, worked each day and came home to the children...... waiting into the evening for Oliver to appear. She knew his condition would not be pleasant. Yet again, she became painfully aware of her situation.

Carrie, for the first time, *truly* realized the futility of hoping that Oliver would change. Mama Eva and Papa Ed and other members of her family had talked to her and tried to convince her that he would not, but Carrie had really *wanted* to believe things could be different.

They had been in the new house for only three months but she could not be a part of this life any more. She needed the support of her family and they were in central Florida almost five hundred miles away.

This time, as Carrie packed her belongings, she knew in her heart that she would be supporting her children, by herself, for many years. However, she also knew the peace it would bring to them. Being away from the influence of drinking and the uncertainty of each day would be worth the sacrifice.

As Carrie prepared to uproot her children, she could not know she was in for a *big surprise,* in the very near future.

* * *

Shortly after Carrie and the children settled in at Mama Eva and Papa Ed's house, they planned a visit to their home state of Alabama.

It was time to see family and old friends and Carrie was excited to accompany them. She had not seen Clara Collier for several years and she had such fond memories of her.

Carrie, did not realize that Clint was home from his military travels. It had been years since she had seen him and they both had been through a lot.

Millie, Clint's wife, had gone to visit her children but the story was….. that she had a *sick sister* she needed to visit. Therefore, she was not with Clint on this occasion.

* * *

Carrie, wore a beautiful, blue dress, which *she* had recently made and it was very becoming to her. Clint, though he had tried, had not been able to keep his eyes off Carrie since she arrived at the old homestead.

As the two approached the kitchen table, to get lemonade and freshly baked oatmeal cookies, Clint gave Carrie a smile and a wink. Surprised, confused and embarrassed, Carrie quickly checked to see if anyone had observed the wink from Clint as she hurried away, trying to conceal her undeniable blush.

"What was that all about?" Carrie wondered.

"Surely he could not still have feelings for me after all these years, especially after what I did to him."

"But then it was not like Clint to be cruel or teasing," she continued …reasoning in her mind.

"Was he trying to let me know he still cares?"

Even if he did, they both knew that it was impossible now. Clint's eyes followed her as she quickly retreated. "Did I offend her?" he wondered, as a puzzled look crossed his face.

As he continued to watch, Clint couldn't help his thoughts.

"Carrie, you look so beautiful today. I wish I could tell you."

Even though their hearts ached, they were married to other people and their belief systems left no room for any advance toward an improper relationship. That had been established a long time ago.

Carrie, found her way to the open back-porch, hoping that in a short time her face would return to its normal color. She found an old rocker, that had seen many years of use and settled down to rest.

She rocked slowly…… letting her mind wander as she looked out over the familiar back yard. Her thoughts quickly drifted back to the days when she and Clint, sat together, on that same porch.....swinging their legs over the splintered edge......enjoying each other's company and planning *their* future together.

"God, that was so long ago."

"What does my life hold in the years I have left?"

"Will I always be alone?"

She listened quietly for an answer, that did not come audibly, but came with an assurance that she had not felt in a long time. Carrie's, small but growing faith could not be mistaken. What had started as the determination of an eight-year-old seeking a ten-cent watch, had developed into the knowledge in the heart of a hurting woman, that as determined and as tough as she was she could not make it all alone.

She realized she needed help..... she needed God.

* * *

Carrie, came home with a determination to return to regular church attendance with her children.

This was a very hard time in the life of her three children and she now realized that she also needed help from God. He would be her strength from this point forward.

The white, wooden church with the bell-tower steeple was just around the corner from where they lived with Mama Eva and Papa Ed.

Pastor Stevens, was the talk of the neighborhood. He, his wife Doris and their two small children, had recently assumed the pastorate of their church. The previous pastor, was retiring following many years of service and recommended Pastor Stevens highly, as his replacement. Although, the church loved the elder pastor for his service to them, hope was high for a fresh approach in ministry to their church and the community.

Darla, had already expressed her desire to be a part of the church activities and Foster, was easily influenced. He followed his sister and his mother's lead and began to attend with them. Loren, was now age three and happy to follow along with the others.

Carrie, found a job working with Mama Eva at her *home-shop* and also, working with an interior decorator in town. She was determined, that this time, she was on her own and the break from Oliver was sure.

My God shall supply all your needs according to
His riches in glory in Christ Jesus...

Phil 4:19

Chapter Six

The fatigue and nausea were continually growing worse, as Carrie struggled to work each day. She tried to brush it off, as *all the tension* she was under, while starting over in a new place. A week later, she could no longer ignore it and a trip to the doctor revealed Carrie's problem.

She was pregnant! "Oh, no… not now," Carrie sighed.

She wondered how she could handle *anything* else right now. When she left Oliver she had no idea that she was pregnant.

"It will be hard enough to provide for the three children I have and how can I ask Mama and Papa Ed to let us stay longer?" She pondered.

After a couple of days, wrestling with the issue, Carrie, shared the news with Mama Eva and Papa Ed. Showing their usual compassion, they assured her she could stay until she had the baby and could find a home of her own.

Carrie, continued working and attending church. As she hoped, over time, she became a valuable part of the church and neighborhood. Everyone was so supportive and the new, young pastor, was one of the kindest men she had ever known. He had good humor and wisdom beyond his years.

She soon began to feel that she and the children were going to be okay!

Oliver, had moved to a town about forty miles away and he occasionally came over to see Carrie and the children. When he heard of her pregnancy, of course, he wanted to use it as a reason to win her back again. Carrie, resisted with determination and this time, she won.

A couple of months later, one of her doctors visits revealed that Carrie, was having *two* babies, not one. What a shock!

Twins! There were no twins in the family that she knew of and everyone was very surprised. Neither were twins a common occurrence in their town, so Carrie quickly became the talk of the neighborhood.

With two babies on the way, family and friends alike were full of suggestions for names and offered their help.....gathering things to accommodate the twins upon their arrival.

Her pregnancy ended early, as expected, and after three days of labor Carrie gave birth to twin girls.....the oldest one Kathryn and the youngest one Karen. It was *her* thirty-sixth birthday. What a birthday present!

There were articles and pictures in the local paper and the twins, born on their mother's birthday, became the big news of the neighborhood and at church. Carrie's head was whirling with excitement. She was the center of attention for the first time in a long time.

It didn't take long, however, for Carrie to realize that caring for two babies could be overwhelming, both physically and financially.....especially when you have three other children.

Karen, came home with Carrie, but Katie, as she was tagged, was underdeveloped and she had to stay in the hospital for one month. She was smaller in weight, had no eyelashes and her eyes resembled those of a frog.

Her look and her size gave Papa Ed a sympathetic heart for her. Katie, became his favorite and he called her "Cricket".

* * *

Darla, now almost fourteen, was expected to add child-care to her other chores of cooking, washing clothes, cleaning house and doing dishes; While also attending high school. She had developed an interest in the music program at church, as well. Darla, had a nice voice like her mother and enjoyed the opportunity to sing.......even if she did get so nervous, she broke out in hives, when performing.

* * *

Foster, was proud of his new baby sisters but unfortunately, at age sixteen, he was still trying to find his way. Oliver, at best, did not express his feelings well and had not been a good role model for Foster. At times, there was *no* father figure in his life and he had not developed the ability to relate to people in a pleasant way.

He was not sure of who he was and became overbearing, insisting that he knew something about everything and how it was supposed to work. You could not convince him otherwise. This made him seem not very bright, when that was not at all the fact. He was just trying to fit in but did not know how. Actually, he had proved, most times, to be correct, but did not possess the determination or cunning that Carrie had passed down to Darla. He had a negative effect on those who he would attempt to convince. People did not know that below that exterior resided the best heart anyone could have.

Foster, was more like his uncle Jeffery and his grandfather, for whom he was named. They were the sensitive gentle natured ones of the family. Foster, was not a good student and had dropped out of school to enlist in the Army.

There was no war at the time and Carrie hoped it would be a good way for him to become *a man* and get an education.......but it did not turn out that way for Foster. Already with inferior feelings, the daily debasement by officers and the other enlisted men became yet another disappointing experience in his life.

* * *

Darla, on the other hand, with her mother's persistence, continued to attend church and at the tender age of sixteen planned to marry John, the young *man* who was to be the steadying force in her life. He was blonde, athletic and quite good-looking. He sported a beautiful tan from his construction work and he was very hard working. He was a man she could depend on........something Darla had not experienced before.

Darla, was very young in age and although experienced in the duties of caring for a house and babies, she certainly was *not* mature in other ways.

Carrie, was concerned that her daughter would end up in the same situation as she had, marrying young and then regretting it. Just as Carrie's own mother had prayed for her, Carrie, prayed for Darla.

* * *

After some time, Carrie, was able to move herself and her three remaining children, to a home of their own. The home was simple and run down, but it proved sufficient and Katie, Karen, and Loren were growing up. Carrie, worked hard and over the next few years she and her children lived in relative peace.

At times, she was very lonely but she remained hopeful

that the life of her children would be better than her life had been to this point. She loved her children and *they* were her life.

God had helped her in ways she had not thought possible and He was not through yet. Carrie was faithful to pray for her family, not thinking of herself.

Oliver, came over occasionally to see Carrie and the children. He was not happy, at all, about the marriage of his daughter. He did not approve of John, even though he didn't really know him and Oliver had done his best to prevent the marriage.

Darla, and John, were married with Foster, walking her down the aisle and Carrie, giving her daughter away at the appropriate time. They had decided that the minister would not ask if anyone had any objections, just in case Oliver appeared at the wedding.

Years later, Oliver had to admit, that although he had not wanted Darla to marry John, he was quite proud of the fact that they were doing so well. The two of them had a nice home and were raising children of their own.

Oliver, measured success by money, as most people do, and he could see that John provided well for his family. The spiritual values, which were being instilled in his grandchildren, were not visible to him and *seemed* unimportant.

* * *

Oliver, had now purchased a modest home and operated a used furniture business, as well as selling vegetables at a roadside stand.

After some time had passed, Carrie decided to give Oliver another chance. He had changed, settling down to a degree as he had grown older. She realized that Karen, Katie and Loren, did not know much about their dad, so she and the children moved into Oliver's home with him, forty miles away. Carrie, still needed to work and still traveled, back and forth to work, each day. She had a good job, which she enjoyed.

Everything seemed *okay* as she prayed and hoped for a good result.

* * *

Much to the entire family's surprise, early on a fall morning, their beloved, Papa Ed had a heart attack, at home, and died within a few minutes. The family and community were shocked and saddened by his loss.

Once again, Eva knew the sorrow of losing a husband. All the family gathered to say goodbye to the man who had become a true father to the fatherless and husband to the widow. He was not necessarily a religious man......but he was a good example of that portion of scripture in the Bible.

Papa Ed, would be missed by *all* his children and especially by his wife, Eva. Strong and independent, she lived out her years alone as she continued to pray for her children and grandchildren. Mama Eva's fingers were now crippled by arthritis. The quilts that had been stitched with love, making memories many years before, had given way to prayers woven on long lonely days as she prayed for her children and grandchildren.

"That is why God is keeping me here," she would say.

There was not a more loving woman than Eva Chamberlain. She had rallied the family over the years, in times of joy and sorrow. Many happy times are remembered at her and Papa Ed's home during the Christmas and Thanksgiving holidays and summer ice-cream freezes. There was never a place to sit and eat. The kitchen was tiny and nothing was convenient but no one even noticed. A*bsolutely nothing* could keep them away.

Family times were special times indeed!

* * *

After a few months it was again obvious, that even though Carrie wished it were different, Oliver had the same basic problems. Karen and Katie, had taken over the nightly job of taking off Oliver's shoes and cleaning his feet. They both disliked it as much as Darla had before them.

One night, Oliver came home drinking and as usual, began an argument. In his anger he shoved Carrie, causing her to fall against the sharp corner of the kitchen wall...... her back hitting with a loud thump. The *immediate* pain was tremendous.

Karen and Katie, who were watching from a safe distance, now ran to help their mother. Carrie, yelled out in pain, noticing that her legs were going numb. She cried as she slide to the floor, unable to stay standing. She sat there weeping, trying to get up.

Katie, seeing her mother's distress, quickly ran out the front door before Oliver could stop her. Her first impulse was to get help. She ran as fast as she could toward the neighbor's house. She was afraid of the dark and it was pitch black that night, with no moon in sight.

Katie, couldn't see where she was going as she stumbled down the street, but her fear for her mother's safety totally filled her mind. She finally reached the neighbor's fence and was fumbling to find the gate, as she cried out for her neighbor to help them.

Just then, out of nowhere Karen appeared, startling Katie. Carrie, had sent her to bring Katie back home. She knew it would be worse if the neighbors became involved.

The girls returned home quickly as their mother had requested. With fear in their eyes, they entered their home, not knowing what their father would do. As they walked in, Oliver walked toward them. In a subdued tone he told them, expressing some degree of regret, to "get their mother to the bedroom and she would be okay."

They helped Carrie down the hall to the small bedroom which they shared and sat with her through the night..... to make sure she was okay. This event had made them more fearful, unsure of how to relate to their father.....and unsure if they even wanted to.

They did remember some good times with their dad, when he took them to the livestock auctions and he even bought them a horse.

They remembered, with amusement, as they returned home one day describing to Carrie how they had tried to bring tiny piglet's home from the auction. Oliver, had put Karen and Katie in the back of his truck to watch them, so they would not get away. As he drove away, the piglets wiggled out of Karen and Katie's arms, jumped out of the truck and ran back to their mother. This happened twice during the trip home and the twins were relieved, when Oliver only laughed at the situation. It was a rare occasion for them to see their dad laugh.

Katie and Karen, tried to stay out of their father's way most of the time. They always hoped that Carrie would be at home when they arrived from school.... not *just* their father. They were always trying to keep things on an even keel.

The twins, just as Darla had before them, inherited Carrie's love of music and began to sing special songs in a church near their home. Carrie, though it was difficult, always made an effort to practice her faith and to pass it along to her children.

Karen and Katie, as well as Darla, have fond memories of Oliver slipping into the back of the church to hear them sing and then he would leave before the service ended. They were small things, but things that meant a lot, because they were rare.

Oliver, was proud of his girls but he did not know how to show them he cared.

Carrie's thoughts lately, in which she weighed the good and the bad, always went back to the drinking, the arguing and the women. The *scale,* which balanced their marriage relationship had more bad than good and like a battle-worn ship was listing to one side.

"I should not have made the move," mused Carrie, as she drove home one day, "but now it's done."

Could she dare uproot her family, yet again?

Carrie did not share her feelings with anyone. Not even Oliver.

Much to her surprise, one day, Oliver came home with a bombshell of his own. One Carrie had not anticipated. He wanted a divorce.

"A divorce?"

Carrie's mind began to whirl so fast, that everything became an instant blur.

"How could *he,* after all these years of begging *me* to return to him, want a divorce?"

She cried often over the next few days and quite frankly became a little angry with God, questioning what He was doing with her life.

Had *she* not been the one to stick it out and give chance after chance to an undeserving man? Hadn't *she* been the one to hold the children together in hard times? *She* had given up *her* home and given Oliver yet another chance. Now, *he* wanted a divorce.

"Why?" demanded Carrie, as she angrily confronted Oliver.

The story was that Oliver had met another woman, as he had many times before. She was a neighbor and spent time with Oliver while Carrie was away at work and the children were at school.

There had been *many* infidelities.

"What was different this time?" Carrie wondered.

This was just another spike that Oliver had driven into

Carrie's heart._

"How could I have been so stupid?" she screamed.

"God, what is going to happen to me?"

Deep inside, even through her pain, Carrie knew that God would not let her down. He had promised. Carrie did not realize it then, but this was just another step that she must take in working out God's plan for her life.

Gathering all her belongings, she and the children moved back to the town where she still worked near Mama Eva. She would make her way a*gain.*

Carrie, told Oliver, "*I* will not get a divorce. I do not believe that is the solution, but I won't object if you do."

She was disappointed that the marriage she had fought to save, so many times....over so many years, would no longer exist.

"After all, anything *she* fought for *that* hard had to succeed. Right?"

It was not a *good* marriage, but it was all she had. However, Carrie realized her strength was gone.

A few years before, on that farmhouse porch in Alabama, God had promised to fight her battles. This was one of those times that Carrie had to relent and let God take control. *She* had no answers.

Within a few weeks, Carrie received the final divorce papers and once again, the finality of it all, became more than she could take.

She sobbed for hours, not being able to hold back her tears of sadness and defeat.

"Had *she* failed, in some way, to show Oliver the love she had promised on their wedding day?"

"What events had led to the failure of her marriage?"

"God please show me the answer and give me the strength I need to raise my children," she begged......as she prayed once again for His help.

* * *

Carrie's daughter, Darla, and her husband John, were now respected members of the community and faithful volunteer workers in their church. Their family was growing with the addition of a new daughter, Marcy and a new son, Ryan. Darla, enjoyed singing with the church choir and John, was teaching a group of young people that adored him.

* * *

Foster, home from the military for a couple of years, had married but was now floundering in that relationship. He had to leave his first love in Korea, where his unit had been stationed. The pretty, young Korean girl loved him for who he was. He was an American, which their culture respected and her expectations were not as high as some girls might have back home in the states.

Foster, was devastated when his medical problems caused him to be sent home before he was able to make contact with her to make the proper arrangements. He wanted her to come home with him. Unfortunately, due to the circumstances, their relationship ended.

Foster's new wife, had brought problems of her own to their relationship and eventually, she was not able to cope with the daily responsibilities of marriage and parenthood. She left Foster and her sons without a word.

They had two boys that needed care and Foster could not do this by himself. In order to keep them in the family, Carrie had no choice. She took Josh and Timmy to live with her. She did not know it then but she would have them for many years, raising them as her own.

* * *

Loren, was losing his way without a father's guidance. He was skipping school and getting into trouble like a lot of teen age boys do. He and a friend took Carrie's checkbook and left town. They went as far as Atlanta, but because of the cold weather and no food, they turned themselves in to the police. Carrie, sent money for a plane ticket and Loren was quickly on his way back home. She was feeling the burden of raising her son alone....being both mother and father.

* * *

Though Carrie loved all her children equally, Karen and Katie were the brightest spot in her life at that time. They were still young and except for their experience with their father, still believed that anything was possible if they decided they wanted to do it.

Carrie, did her best but she could not work full time to meet the needs of the family and keep a constant watch on her children. She prayed for them, worked hard and as always, gave her very best.

* * *

Carrie, was surprised, a few months after the divorce, to hear from Oliver. The woman he had intended to marry had disappointed him in *some* way and he had decided that she was *not* what he wanted.

He "realized that he had made a mistake," in divorcing Carrie.

She was hesitant at first to listen to his story. Nevertheless, something in her heart pulled her to him. Was it God's love reaching out to Oliver through Carrie?

She decided to, at least, talk with him and over the next

few weeks, once again, the love of the past was rekindled. She discovered that Oliver was more understanding of her needs and she had finally forgiven him of his many shortcomings.

Much to Carrie's delight, she found that he was now attending church and there was a noticeable change in his life. Carrie's heart could sense the change and even the children could see the difference.

Loren, had recently married and now, Karen and Katie were the only children still living at home. Soon they would be graduating from high school and their hope was to attend college.

When Carrie decided to marry Oliver, all over again, she consulted with the twins to see how they felt. Even seeing the difference in their father, they still had an underlying fear that he had not changed.....enough.

"Mother, we understand that you love Daddy and want to do what is right, but we cannot live with him again. We hope you understand."

They knew their mother had already sacrificed so much for them and they offered to stay with Mama Eva, until they finished their last year of school, so Carrie would be free to live with Oliver.

Carrie, being the great mom she was, understood their feelings and the decision was made to marry Oliver, but she would remain in her home there for one year, until the twins graduated. She would see Oliver on the weekends.

After just a few months, Carrie remarried Oliver in the church *he* was attending. The same church where he had slipped into the back pew to see his daughters sing. On this day, all three of them sang for his wedding. Oliver, was smiling from ear to ear.

* * *

Carrie, continued to live in her trailer home near Mama Eva with Karen and Katie, and Foster's children, Josh and Timmy. Oliver, still lived in their home forty miles away.

They saw each other on weekends, while Carrie, continued to work as a seamstress and Oliver, continued to sell second-hand furniture, as well as vegetables and fruit from his roadside stand.

He was only sixty-two years old, but his health was failing from the years of abuse to his body. The extra weight he carried made it hard for him to breathe when lying down. His life had been spent in wrong pursuits and bad decisions, except for the day he married Carrie. Oliver had not changed but better yet, *God* had changed him.

After his conversion, he told Carrie….

"I really don't know how you put up with me over the years, but I'm so glad you did."

He realized that no one else would have stayed with him and he loved her for it. They were experiencing the best time of their life, as man and wife, since the very early years of their marriage.

The dreams they had many years ago had not worked out, but somehow here they were together, looking to their remaining years with *new* dreams and hopes.

Oliver, had a sensitive side that was hidden to most people, but now it was able to bloom. He had a spiritual awareness that some are never able to achieve.

* * *

Foster's children, Josh and Tim, were enjoyable to have around. Oliver, became very protective of them, especially when their mother would return to cause trouble, or attempt to take them away.

She had been declared an unfit mother. The courts decided it would be best for the boys not to be with their parents and Carrie had assumed responsibility for the pair, as we know, a few years before.

Carrie, worked even harder to make a home on a very small budget for her girls, who were now seniors in high-school and her two grandsons.

She and Oliver looked forward to the weekends when they were able to be together. Their *new* love was blossoming and though Oliver was no singer, he could be found *trying* to sing his favorite love song "Together Again," which spoke of a couple making a new start. Carrie, couldn't help but smile at his attempt. Oliver, had no talent for singing, but of course he knew that.

He was thankful for Carrie and knew she was someone he did not deserve and *she* was becoming more aware of the wonderful changes in his life.

* * *

One Saturday morning early in September, Carrie, woke with a start. Her heart felt as if it would pound out of her chest and she quickly checked to see if Oliver was in bed beside her. She found him quietly looking at the ceiling, waiting for her to wake up. He was thinking how lucky he was to have Carrie by his side.

"Good morning," said Carrie, trying to hide her fear. However, Oliver could tell that something was not right.

"What's wrong?" he asked.

"I had a dream about you," she replied quietly.

"Oh?" Oliver questioned.

He could see the concern in her eyes.

"Tell me," he said.

"Are you sure you want to hear," Carrie whispered.

"Go on," Oliver prompted.

Carefully, as if to recollect every detail, Carrie began to relay her dream to Oliver.

She had found herself in a yard with Oliver and two other women. One of the women had two children with her and the other was alone. They were having an argument over which one of them Oliver was to leave with on that day.

Carrie, interrupting at one point, told the women that she did not know what claim they had on Oliver but she and Oliver had been re-married on July 28th and that he was her husband.

She turned to Oliver and said, "I am leaving if you want to come with me."

Oliver, not lingering, had quickly followed behind Carrie as she walked away. Carrie, then heard an unexpected sound and turned back to see Oliver thrashing around in a small pool of water. Then, to her surprise, she heard sirens blaring in the distance growing louder as each second passed. They were coming closer.

As she turned forward, she was suddenly, without warning, caught up in a giant whirlwind and softly set down in a beautiful and peaceful place.

As she looked, she saw a tall and beautifully majestic gate with spires rising to the heavens. To her side, she saw two men dressed in white, with hoods over their heads, walking by a stream of water just a few yards away.

As she stood wondering who they were, they approached her and asked,

"What are you doing here?"

Carrie replied, as she stretched her cupped hands toward them,

"I came to return something that I borrowed."

As they were speaking, the gates opened and a helicopter flew from behind her entering through the gate.

She began to walk through the gate attempting to follow the helicopter, but the men spoke again saying, "No, you cannot go in."

"Yes, I can!" Carrie cried loudly.

"No, it's not your time" they insisted gently.

She continued to watch as the helicopter disappeared and the gates closed, obscuring her view. The gates were large and beautiful with jewel-like stones.

Just as quickly as she had been transported there, she was again transported, by the same whirlwind, back to the place from which she had been taken.

Oliver was not there.

As Carrie quietly finished her story, she saw Oliver's body go limp. His face had grown pale as Carrie's word picture unfolded before him. He knew, with inner clarity, that this dream was about his *death.*

After a long, silent pause.....Oliver said, trying not to show what he really felt,

"Well, it was just a dream. Let's get up and get some breakfast."

In reality, Oliver was greatly shaken by the event, but did not want to cause Carrie any more alarm than she already felt.

Quietly, they went about the tasks of the day as they each privately reflected on the meaning of Carrie's dream.

Watching Josh and Tim, playing and laughing as the day faded into night, kept them *busy* focusing on living and not worrying about the future. But each held the dream in their hearts.

Call to me and I will answer you,
and I will tell you great and mighty things,
which you do not know…

Jeremiah 33:3

Chapter Seven

The year was passing quickly and Karen and Katie, were growing into lovely young women. They had just graduated from high school.....and had their eyes set on college.

Carrie's support was limited, financially, but she did support her girls anyway she could. They inquired about government grants and loans which were available to young students. But special circumstances would be needed, to make the difference in the money you could get.

Karen and Katie, had no *special circumstances* to go along with their request and Carrie knew, that after the bills were paid there was no money left.

The twins, had begun working earlier that summer to make money for college. With the few dollars they had, in late August..... they took a step of faith.

Karen, had a lovely voice and loved to sing. She wanted to major in Music with teaching as a secondary focus. Katie, was also interested in teaching but approached it from the elementary education angle instead of music.

Karen and Katie, were the first of Carrie's children to *want* to go to college. They were accomplishing something, which to this point, was unheard of in the Wilkins family.

Carrie and Oliver were very proud of them and their determination to succeed.

* * *

On a Friday evening, just a few weeks before Karen and Katie were to enter college, Carrie was making her weekend trip to see Oliver. She asked all three of her daughters to go with her to see their dad. For some reason, she felt it was important.

As the evening progressed, the girls were amazed at the *good* changes they saw in their dad. Although Darla had good memories of personal conversations with her Dad, it was the first time Karen and Katie could remember having a pleasant talk with him. They all could see that God had been at work in his life

When they were ready to leave, Oliver, looked at his daughters and showing an unusual concern for Carrie said to them…

"You all take care of your mother."

Hugs, from his three girls, put a smile on Oliver's face and he watched them leave the room, with the knowledge that he would most likely not see them again.

* * *

The courts had recently decided to place Josh and Tim in state foster homes and thus relieve Carrie and Oliver of their daily care. Carrie, had kept them for several years and been a mother to them. Now, it was time for someone else to help.

It was heart wrenching for Carrie and Oliver, as well as Josh and Tim. They missed each other very much but *seemingly,* it was better for the children to go and live with Carrie's sister, Maggie, and her husband. Bill's business had prospered in the last few years and they were doing well financially. They had a home much too large for just the two of them and they were happy to take the boys for a while. They even spoke of adoption.

Unfortunately as time passed, due to Bill and Maggie's health, they were not able to carry through with this plan and when Josh and Tim were in their early teen years, they were sent back to their father, who lived in Georgia, with yet another new wife.

* * *

With the boys gone and the twins in college, Carrie, was now alone in her trailer home during the week.....but not for long. She was in the process of packing and making arrangements to move back in with Oliver. She had now fulfilled her promise to the twins, to wait one year until they left for college.

A week later, on the second weekend of September, there was a Friday Night Fish Fry at church that Carrie wanted to attend. She would say goodbye to everyone before she made her move. She and Oliver had decided, for that weekend, she would see him on Saturday and Sunday. Besides, after one more week they would be together all the time.

Carrie, knew that Oliver had a medical test scheduled on Friday, but they were not expecting to know the results until the following week. He had been having difficulty breathing and several other worrisome symptoms and the doctor would be looking for the *root* cause of his problems.

On Saturday morning, Carrie set out to see Oliver. She was thinking of her family and what she had to do for the weekend and thankful, unlike times past, that she was *actually* looking forward to seeing Oliver.

This was a big difference from the time she had dreaded

the drinking and late nights.... wondering where he was.

* * *

When she arrived at their home, she could not find Oliver anywhere. She asked the neighbors but they didn't know and they had not seen him all day.

Carrie, knew that Oliver's test had been scheduled for Friday and she thought maybe the doctor had kept him overnight at the hospital, for some reason. The fact, that he was not there....... made her quite uneasy.

When she called the hospital, she could not believe what they were telling her. Part of the test was an injection of dye in order to follow its course through his body and get the result for the test. Oliver had asked them not to lie him down completely, because that made his breathing worse.

They started the test, as scheduled, but a few minutes into the testing something went seriously wrong. Oliver, had an allergic reaction to the medication they used. He immediately began to gasp for air and struggled to set himself upright on the table. Seeing his adverse reaction, the doctors immediately started measures to relieve him.

"Please find my wife," Oliver begged, as best he could.

His breaths were short and his voice raspy and harsh as he labored to speak. The nurse settled him down and gave him a *new* medication to counteract the dye, which had caused his negative reaction.

Carrie, also learned that the hospital officials sent the police to notify her but she was at the church Fish Fry, and not at home, when they came. Oliver, died during the night. He knew that his death was near and he wanted to see Carrie one more time.

Carrie, could not believe her ears.

"How could I not know?"

"Oh Oliver, I should have been there," Carrie sobbed.

Her heart was torn in pieces.

"How could I have left him to die alone?" she thought.

"Oh Oliver, things should have been different," she screamed over and over again.

Tormenting tears of sorrow streamed down her face for many hours, as she comprehended what had happened, just when they had just gotten their life together. Oliver, was *finally* going to church, being a loving man and had become the familiar Oliver of their early years.

"Why? Why now God?" Carrie demanded, sternly.

As the hours passed, Carrie remembered that a couple of weeks before, Darla, Katie and Karen had seen their dad. She also remembered that he had made a point of telling them to...... "Take care of your mother."

Carrie, found out later that Oliver told several people he was going to die. Although we all are going to die sometime, his inference was that he *knew* he would die soon.

She remembered the dream that had awaken her, earlier that month as she lay by Oliver, as well as the soberness they had felt on that day. It was still vivid in her mind.

She thought at the time, that it was more likely a vision than a dream. She had certainly not forgotten it. In fact, she would remember it all of her life, just as if it were yesterday. Carrie's thoughts became overwhelming.

"Thank God that He had found Oliver before the day of his death."

"Thank God that He had restored their relationship, after all the years of unhappiness they had experienced because of their selfish wishes and desires.

"Thank God that she had a family on which she could lean at this time." God, was *good* after all.

The young woman, that sat on that farmhouse porch in Alabama, telling God that she needed help, had found Him faithful in her life......over and over again.

"He, would be faithful now," she had no doubt.

* * *

The next few days were a blur. The family was notified, funeral arrangements were made and Oliver was laid in the ground. The burial plot, which Carrie purchased for Oliver, included a place for her to be by his side in the future.

It broke the hearts of all Carrie's children, to see her sobbing over the grave of Oliver.

They too, questioned, "Why now?"

Even though they all had suffered many unhappy moments, they knew that their father had changed and their mother was very hurt at his death.

Darla, was not without bad memories and experiences that she needed to work through. However, she had felt a bond of love with her father, that she could not explain, in *spite* of his shortcomings. She was happy that he had found his way home to God.

Karen and Katie, expressed openly that their feelings of sorrow were for their mother and not feelings of loss of their father. Hurts can run deep and it takes time to heal even if you have forgiven.

The twins, knew Oliver had changed and they were sorry they had created the conditions that made their mother stay with *them* during the last year, instead of with Oliver. Of course, they never dreamed this would happen.

Oliver and Carrie, had learned that a life spent in the pursuit of your own desires, does not make for a happy ever after, even when you turn your life around. It is impossible to dig up all the seeds you have sown. Sometimes hurts are too deep to heal quickly. Only time and God can do that.

Thankfully, God loved Oliver enough to *forgive and forget*. We humans however, have a memory and we have to work through those hard memories to find forgiveness for others and ourselves.

* * *

Loren and Foster, like their father, did not express emotion outwardly but they too found a well-defined sense of loss in their hearts.

Did they realize that they, themselves, were sowing seeds which would one day be harvested? Seeds, that would need special forgiveness from those who loved them.

Their own lives needed to be brought into order and submission to God. There was still hope, especially on Carrie's part, that this would become a reality in their lives.

She, as always, had *unrelenting hope.*

* * *

Over the next few weeks, Carrie found herself in constant change. Josh and Tim had recently moved out, Karen and Katie left for college and Oliver had passed away. Her daughter, Darla, and her family were close by and of course, there was Mama Eva, her constant guiding force and special friend.

Carrie, realized she needed to get back to normal, whatever normal was. She returned to work and began to build her life, very aware of the fact that she was now *alone.*

Oliver's death, had created the special circumstances in the twins life that made it possible for them to receive funds to go to college. A small portion from Social Security and grants and loans helped to them to achieve their dream.

"Funny how things work out," Carrie thought. Of course, God knew. In an unexpected way, Oliver was still giving to them after his death, but this time in a *positive* way.

Darla, tried to spend extra time with her mom, but caring for her own four children and her husband John, as well as holding down a job made it impossible for her to be there as much as she would like.

Carrie, seemed *fine* outwardly, to her family and friends, but she had her share of sad moments, alone in private.

She had no thought of *her* future at this time, but she stayed the course, doing what she had to do. She was working and helping keep her girls in school. They were the last of her children who were still financially dependent on her.

She was almost there. She had worked. God had blessed and she was surviving on her own. What the future held...... she did not know.

* * *

Carrie, was at her kitchen table one evening, writing bills, when she received a call from Mama Eva. The words she heard took her by *total* surprise.

"You are kidding!" Carrie exclaimed.

"No," said Mama Eva, "he called here because he didn't have your number. He wants to get in touch with you but he didn't say why. He left *his* number and he wants you to call him at eight o'clock this evening."

Carrie's heart beat faster at the prospect.

"What could he want?"

It was not as if she hadn't thought of him occasionally, but she certainly did not expect to hear from him.

Clint's mother, Clara, had called Mama Eva a few months ago when Clint's wife passed away.

Carrie, remembered that she had been sad for Clint, because she had gone through the same experience with Oliver just a few months before. But she did not let her mind go into what might have been. Oliver's death was still too fresh at that time.

Her mind began to race with imaginations, but soon, Carrie came to the decision that it would be okay to return his call.

She resisted the idea that it was anything *personal.* There could be hundreds of reasons that he wanted to get in touch with her.

* * *

Clint, sat in his well-worn, plaid, recliner in the den of his modest South Georgia home. He found himself a little nervous with anticipation as he awaited Carrie's call. On the other hand, would she call at all?

Although family gatherings had brought them together on occasion over the years, it had been quite some time since they had seen each other.

He heard that Oliver had passed away five months before but he had not attended the funeral or even sent a sympathy card. At that time, he was in the process of caring for Millie as she fought for her life against the ravages of cancer.

He and Millie had lived a *good* life together. They had seen the world, they had great neighbors and they lived in the same community for all the years of their marriage. That is, when they were not traveling with the military.

They never had children of their own but over the years, had visited Millie's children in order to be a small part of their lives. Millie's wish remained…..not to acknowledge them to anyone. Close friends and neighbors were shocked to find out that Millie had two children when they attended their mother's funeral.

Her fight against cancer had ended a couple of months before and now, Clint was alone.

Not surprisingly, his reflections as he wondered about the brevity of life, included Carrie. She *was* the love of his life, that left him for Oliver many years ago.

He had never felt bitter or stopped loving Carrie. He held her with great tenderness in his heart all those years.

* * *

Clint, quickly looked at the clock. It was seven forty-five. "Why hadn't he asked her to call earlier, then all the suspense would be over?"

"Would she call at all?"

He figured that if she did *not* call, that would be an answer to him that she was not interested.

"She must have heard that Millie is gone," Clint reasoned.

On the other hand, maybe she would think it was too *soon* for him to be calling her.

Clint, was shocked back into reality when the phone rang.

He again looked at the clock. It was exactly eight o'clock.

"Was it Carrie?" he wondered.

It could have been one of the widow women from the church, who had called him frequently over the last few days.

Clint, still very handsome, was now an eligible bachelor and had become especially interesting to a couple of the women at his church. Clint, was not interested in them and viewed them as a nuisance, but he was always kind to them. Maybe this seemed to them somewhat of an encouragement. Whatever the reasons for their calls, Clint was thinking of only *one* person right now.

* * *

Carrie, was sitting on "pins and needles," waiting for the phone to be answered. It had rung three times now.

She felt a little *sting* in her heart as she wondered if he had gone out, or worse, had forgotten that he had even asked her to call. A feeling of fear began to make its way into her mind.

Her question was answered however, when a familiar voice from the past finally said,

"Hello Carrie ....I'm so glad you called."

The two of them talked for over an hour carefully navigating their way through small talk and with a new sense of wonder, they finished their conversation with Clint's question that he asked with a boyish charm.

"Can I write you and call again soon?"

"Yes," Carrie had replied without hesitation.

"I would like that. Well, ...Goodnight."

As they hung up the telephone, they both had the unmistakable feeling that the *old love* they had shared years ago still had hope.

Through the embers of the pain in both their lives, *could* a new love be established? Only God knew.

* * *

Clint, sighed confidently as he sat back in his recliner and glanced around the room.

"That went pretty well," he thought.

In his mind, he replayed the conversation with Carrie, until his eyes came to rest on Millie's picture, sitting on the little bureau which was tucked tightly in the corner of the small den. He quietly remembered the last few weeks of Millie's life when she was suffering so much from the disease that finally took her away.

He had cared for her with love and kindness over those weeks and months and he thanked her for their life together.

No doubt, at some point during the years of their marriage, she had become aware of the lingering feelings that Clint had for Carrie, his childhood sweetheart.

Millie's thoughts on her deathbed were not for herself, but for Clint. She knew he did not do well, living alone, and had never been one to take on the regular household chores, such as cleaning and cooking.

That had been *her job* and with no other obvious

hobbies or talents, she had put everything into taking care of their home.... and kept it shining. It was always welcoming for their friends, their neighbors, and her dear Clint.

"Clint, I know the time is short and I want you to do something for me," Millie whispered.

"Anything Millie," Clint replied.

"When I am gone, I want you to go and get your old sweetheart to be with you."

Millie, knew of course that Carrie's husband, Oliver, had passed away a few months before.

Clint, taken by surprise, quickly raised his eyes to meet Millie's. Her eyes looked very tired.

They showed the pain she was feeling from the cancer and the idea of leaving him. She wanted him to be happy and she knew that Carrie could make him happy.

"Don't talk like that Millie. You're going to be okay."

"No, Clint," she replied grasping for another ounce of strength.

"We both know I'm not. I don't want you to be alone. I know you still have feelings for Carrie."

The lingering look between them needed no words. They *both* knew it was true.

Millie, appreciated the life they had shared and now she wanted to leave him, knowing that he would be happy.

"Thank you Millie," whispered Clint.

Those words were a comfort to her and Clint as well. Moments later, while still holding Clint's hand, she slipped from life to death, leaving behind the man she had loved for many years.

* * *

As Carrie hung up the phone, her heart was as light as a feather and she felt an excitement she had not known for years.

The last few months had been so lonely. She had gone through the separation from her grandchildren, her daughters leaving for college and of course, Oliver's death.

As Carrie continued to reflect on the last few months, she did not realize that her life had been orchestrated for her to be available and free from responsibilities when Clint called. She couldn't help but feel the excitement of a young girl at the thought of Clint in her life again.

On the first ring, Carrie picked up the phone and heard Mama Eva asking,

"Well, did you call?"

Carrie, had expressed to her mother her feelings of anxiety about calling Clint, not knowing what he wanted. She had silently *hoped*, but could not be sure, that he wanted to see her.

"Yes! I called," Carrie squealed. Her excitement was overwhelming.

"How did it go Carrie?" inquired Mama Eva, with a lilt in her voice that was so like her. She could read her daughter well and she knew from Carrie's response that she was very excited.

"Mama, he wants to call again soon. He also wants to come down in a couple of weeks to see me."

"Oh?".... said Mama Eva with a half-understanding, half-questioning tone.

Teasingly she asked, "What does he want?"

"I don't know for sure," replied Carrie, not able to conceal the fact that she was beside herself with hope.

Carrie, was now in her early fifties and Mama Eva, in her late seventies with solid white-hair and many character lines. But there they were, giggling together....sharing the moment.... mother and daughter.

It was the same emotion a young girl and her mother might share when a special man "*comes calling,*" for the first time. It brought back memories of times long ago.

Each of them, let their mind ponder the question Mama Eva had posed...... and they each had their own ideas about what the answer would be. Anyway, they could dream, and they did.

* * *

Later that evening, Carrie, let her mind wander back over the memories she had stored up, good and bad. Her life had been hard to this point......very hard.

She had no regrets for keeping her vows and her promise to God, to stay with a bad marriage until it became good. *He* had kept His promise also, to take care of her and reward her with a chance for a new life. And what a new life it was.

Over the next few months the calls, the letters, Clint's visits, and Carrie's hopeful anticipation of his intentions, ended. Clint popped the question!

"Carrie, you may not know this, but I have loved you my whole life. I am so happy that our paths have crossed again and that God has put us in circumstances where we can *share* what is left of our lives."

"Carrie, will you marry me?"

"Yes, yes, yes!" Carrie whispered, with an eager, but girlish, shyness.

It was as if it were the first time she had been asked. She felt a familiar blush on her face, as Clint took her hand. He smiled tenderly as he hugged Carrie with a firm, but gentle caress. He did not want her to get away again. This time he would see to it. Clint, would take care of his beloved and give her a *good* life from this day forward.

After a few short months, Carrie married her *first* love in a garden wedding, in John and Darla's back yard.

The young preacher was there, but he was not so young now. Time had passed since his automobile accident, which left him crippled and walking with a brace and cane. However, he had no trouble performing *this* wedding and he expressed his happiness for Carrie's new future.

Clara and Eva, were dressed in their finery, with obvious smiles of satisfaction. They had been friends over all these years and nothing could have made them happier than the marriage of their children. Admiring glances, from one to the other, told the story of how they had hoped for this day.

Karen, Katie and Darla, sang the songs Carrie had chosen. Clint, gazed at Carrie as she left the enclosed porch and began her walk across the lawn to meet him. He wondered if it could be true. Long ago, on a Saturday morning, he had watched her.... as she walked down a sidewalk, around a street corner and out of his life. He had given up all hope of a life together and now, here she was, walking toward him with love in her eyes.

As she walked, Carrie's eyes met Clint's.

"This is my handsome love of long ago," she thought.

"Thank you, God, for bringing Clint back into my life."

Carrie, was radiant with happiness, as she walked across the lawn to take Clint's strong hand and become Mrs. Clint Collier. Who could have known, that now, in God's timing, He would bless them in this way.

Carrie, had discussed her plans with all five of her children making sure that none of them had any objection to the marriage.

As she and Clint, joined hands and promised to love honor and cherish, they meant it with all their hearts. "How blessed we are," they whispered. Each, had a smile on their face that the other quickly read with loving understanding.

Their dreams had come true.

Do not urge me to leave you or turn back....for where you go I will go and where you lodge I will lodge...Your people will be my people and your God my God...

Ruth 1:16

Chapter Eight

As Carrie looked back, family and friends were smiling and waving. She could hardly believe it was true. Surely, it was a dream and she would soon wake up to the reality of *her* life.

Clint, was beaming as he opened the car door for Carrie. He helped his new bride, as she lifted the skirt of her pink-chiffon wedding gown into the seat beside her.

The car was decorated to the hilt, as if for *young* newly weds. Ribbons and streamers, with cans attached, bounced gaily behind the car. The words, proclaiming "Just Married," were quite visible, as they pulled away from Darla and John's home.

"Could it be true," they wondered, "that the love that lasted, however dimly at times, for over thirty-five years, could now be expressed?"

"They were now man and wife!"

Clint and Carrie, drove away slowly, fearing they would awake from the wonderful *dream* they were experiencing.

The next few days were fresh and exciting, as they spent time in a little cottage by the river, which Carrie had carefully picked for their honeymoon.

It was now time to return and pack up Carrie's things. Carrie, said goodbye to children, family and friends. Then, they left for Clint's home in Georgia. There they would begin *their* new life. God, had given them a *second chance*. They wanted to get it right!

* * *

Carrie, was more than a little apprehensive at the prospect of meeting Clint's friends and neighbors.

She was a private person to some extent and it always took Carrie time to *warm up* to new people.

"What will they think of me?" she thought.

"How will they feel about a new person living in Millie's house?"

As the feelings began to overwhelm her, worry began to show on Carrie's brow.

"What's wrong?" Clint asked, as they turned onto the street which he called home.

He drove intentionally slow, as he studied Carrie's expression. In a moment, they arrived at Clint's home. It had white clapboard shingles, black window shutters and a little front porch, featuring a picture window and a swing. The homes on the street were neatly situated and very much alike, except for the different colors of shutters.

Those front porches, were places where you could sit and see your neighbors taking an evening stroll. They would wave hello.....even if they didn't know you.

The picture windows, reflected the warmness of the neighborhood as it let in the sunlight and extended an unwritten invitation to "stop in" for iced tea or coffee....depending on the season.

Carrie, noticed that a variety of flowers were in full bloom in the front yards. She had a special love for flowers and gardens.

The butterflies in Carrie's stomach grew more evident as the car pulled onto the long driveway, leading to the covered parking area at the back of Clint's home. From there, you could see the trees filling his backyard. There was a fig tree near the house and tall pines on the rear of the property. She felt as if one could disappear into them, finding a place of refuge where you could think and ponder life's issues.

Next, Carrie noticed a swing near the house that showed signs of wear from much use.

"I'm just a little nervous," said Carrie, finally answering Clint's question.

Clint's next-door neighbors, for the last thirty years, were sitting in their back yard and they waved a welcome as he and Carrie opened the car door.

"Don't worry, they are going to love you," Clint reasured her.

Millie, had been an attractive woman, brown-haired, with comely features and Carrie, *knew* that the years of hard work and worry had taken a toll on her body. After all, she was now fifty-three years old.

With little more than one-hundred pounds on her small frame, Carrie, seemed slight and shy as she shook the hand of her new neighbors. The days of her youthful beauty had diminished somewhat, but her sparkling brown eyes, which could look into your soul, had not changed.

Carrie, carefully studied the faces of Boyd and Trudy Cunningham, hoping to get a glimpse of their thoughts.

Boyd was short, but handsome, and a southern gentleman as you would expect. His years had added that little bulge around the waistline, that surely had been trim at one time.

"Nice to meet ya'll," he said, as he extended his hand to Carrie.

Carrie's gaze, quickly turned to Trudy, with her flame red hair.....which Carrie questioned as her *true* color, and tender blue eyes that made her quite striking. Her strong, southern accent was so charming and had a soothing effect, as the words fell from her lips like syrup pouring from a bottle, thick and slow.

Trudy, quickly put Carrie at ease by her kind nature and the true friendship she offered.

"We have been waiting for you, Carrie. I have dinner prepared if you would like to join us?"

Clint, noticing Carrie's shyness, quickly accepted the invitation and he and Carrie joined the Cunningham's for a dinner of fried chicken, potato salad and coconut cake, a *southern* specialty.

After a polite period of time, Carrie and Clint excused themselves and went to bed, very tired from their journey.

Carrie, felt a little strange in her new surroundings, but happy, as she drifted off to sleep.

* * *

Early the next morning, she woke with a start. Glancing around the room, she found it very unfamiliar. She had to be up to go to work and wondered what time it was. Still groggy, she turned slowly and saw Clint beside her in the mahogany, spindle bed. It didn't take long for her to remember where she was, even though it still seemed like a dream.

Across the small room, she saw the matching mahogany dresser with pictures of Millie and Clint when they were younger. They were held snuggly in a picture frame, which they had purchased during their stay in Japan.

The small bedroom also had two windows, with Venetian blinds and curtains that were not very impressive. They were one of the first things Carrie noticed. Her many years as a professional seamstress had produced in her a critical eye. She found herself *already* thinking of how she could improve the situation and quickly formed some ideas.

Soon, Clint was awake and he turned to look at Carrie.

She was still in awe of what had transpired in their lives. Here she was, with the person she would later recall as the love of her life. With the quick wink......which Clint always loved to give, he said with a lilt in his voice...... "Good morning Mrs. Collier."

Carrie, blushed and said shyly, "Good morning Mr. Collier."

"It is very nice to hear him call me Mrs. *Collier*," she thought.

Giving a quick smile, Carrie asked... "What would you like for breakfast Mr. Collier?" She laughed gently, enjoying the moment as they tossed the name back and forth.

It had been a few years since she had the luxury of *time* to cook a *nice* breakfast. She would make homemade biscuits, (a little flat with crisp edges) bacon and scrambled eggs with red eye gravy, Southern style. Just a few days before she had discovered *that* was Clint's favorite.

Carrie, was very excited as she began to make her way around the kitchen. Clint, had lived alone for a few months now and grocery shopping had not been a priority, or a particular ambition on his part.

Oh, he had survived, but cooking was not one of his strong points and he was really looking forward to a home cooked meal.

Carrie, was relieved to find flour, milk, eggs and bacon and she began to put together the first breakfast for her new husband.

* * *

Clint, was also an *early* riser, she observed. One of the first things he did each day was to walk around inspecting his yard. After all, someone might have come during the night and disturbed something. In that case, he might need to rearrange things or put them back in place.

Today he was showered, shaved and ready for the day quite early. With a few words to Carrie, he began to survey his property.

Her new husband was still a *working man* and lived on a regiment, which was a carry over from his days in the military. That same military training had instilled in him a desire to have everything in order, which was evident in his appearance *and* his home.

Carrie, on the other hand, had always prized cleanliness but raising five children and having several grandchildren around most of the time, had made her more tolerant of a little dirt and clutter.

She proudly watched him as he walked the property with a spring in his step. He was at home and comfortable with his surroundings.

However, Carrie realized that it would take a while for her to call the house, in which she found herself, *home.* She was with Clint and that was all that mattered right now.

"Breakfast is ready," Carrie said cheerfully as Clint came through the screen door. After a quick embrace, they sat down, happy to be together and said a prayer of thankfulness.

* * *

Days and weeks went by with Carrie making small changes, here and there, to suit her style and making the house new for her *and* for Clint. She wanted to replace the things that reminded him of his life with Millie and the sorrow of her death. After all, it was not that long ago. Millie, had been gone for only eight months and now another woman was in the house. Carrie, wanted to be considerate but she also wanted to make Clint's house *her* home.

Over the next few months, she sewed new curtains for the kitchen, new drapes for the living room and began making a flower arrangement for the dining table. She tried not to cause Clint any alarm and moved slowly. Clint, had become comfortable with his home as it was.

The yard was Clint's to care for, but Carrie loved flowers and soon began to use her design ability to plant flowers in the yard. They were a beauty to behold! All kinds of flowers were there to enjoy and could easily have won a landscape award for flower gardens. Carrie's favorite past time *became* working in her garden.

As newly weds, Carrie and Clint had some adjusting to do. They were mature people when they married and each of them had formed ideas and opinions from their previous relationships ......that would need to be *tailored,* for this one.

* * *

On one particular day, Carrie was busy sewing dresses and drapes to her hearts content. Clint, had taken notice that the house was a little untidy with fabric scraps and threads on the floor; As well as the ironing board, *upright*, for ironing seams, as her sewing projects progressed.

Those things, as well as the floral wire and a little dirt tracked in from the flower garden, did not escape his careful eyes.

Clint, in all sincerity made an unintentional mistake. He mentioned to Carrie that the house was not quite as immaculate as he was used to, along with a couple of other things that he found different. Clint, soon found out that his *sweet* Carrie had a fiery side.

As much as Carrie loved Clint, he had to realize that she was a woman who was independent in many ways. She had learned to make it on her own, with no help, on a shoestring budget for many years now. She had developed her own style of keeping a home and she let him know, that she did not appreciate him comparing her with Millie..... particularly not Millie.

Yes, Millie had been a fastidious housekeeper but she had not exhibited any other talents or interests, nor did she ever work outside the home. She had enjoyed a comfortable life, with every thing she needed supplied by her husband.

Carrie, feeling a little offended, retorted that "she was not Millie," and she had "her own way of doing things!" She was Carrie and she would "never be Millie!"

Clint, was surprised at Carrie's response and realized what he had done. He was instantly sorry for his words. How could he have compared her to anyone? She was the *love* he had waited for all his life. He quickly and gently, let Carrie know that he did not expect her to be like Millie and she was loved and valued for who she was.

Yes.....he had forgotten about Carrie's circumstances before they were married. Carrie, had learned from the hard knocks and sorrows in her life to "take the bull by the horns," and make things happen. Necessity was Carrie's teacher and she had learned well.

It took a little while for Clint to come to terms with the bold, new, wife he had in his home. However, he enjoyed learning. Soon the love they shared quickly melted any hurt feelings. They understood each other. They loved each other.

* * *

Over the next few months, Carrie met all the neighbors and Clint's friends at the church he had attended for many years. She was well accepted and loved for *her* caring ways and it was not long before Clint's friends were her friends too.

Every spring, as was *his* custom, she and Clint planted a vegetable garden. They used a small piece of ground, which belonged to one of his friends down the street. It had been a long time since Clint and Carrie had the opportunity to bring back a glimpse of their *young* life and love, which began so many years ago. As they worked side by side, they could *see* themselves back on the farm as young lovers.

Carrie, for the *first* time, did not have to wonder where the next food was coming from, or if she could make the rent payment that month. She did not have to wonder if her husband was coming home that night. Neither did she wonder about his faithfulness to her. In fact, when he was missing she knew exactly where he was. A little utility shed behind their home had become the place where Clint would go to meet God. The old metal, spring-chair was his favorite. He would sit and read his Bible and pray.

That was Carrie's only competition. What a blessing! God had been so good and more faithful to *her* than she had been to Him.

Oliver, had lived the last few months of his life as a caring man, *forgiven* for his past. However, nothing could take the place of the untarnished love that she experienced with Clint.

* * *

Darla and John, came to visit often and quickly became "special" to Clint. He and John became close friends. Clint, did not have children of his own and due to the forbidden circumstances, was never very close with Millie's children.

Carrie's five children, would come to know Clint as a very valued member of their family. He won their hearts and *proved* to be God's choice for their mother. With her children, he found the opportunity to be a father and a very good one at that!

* * *

Karen and Katie, returned from college that summer to a *new* home. They found jobs right away, to help pay for next year's tuition.

Clint, would lovingly refer to the twins as "The Queens."

There was a reason.

Like many young adults, who have been away in college, they conveniently forgot the fact that they were still part of the family, in *everyway.* And when they returned home, they acted like they were guests with guest *privileges.* They did not make a point of helping Carrie with the house work and they stayed out..... late at night .....not letting Carrie know where they were.

Clint and Carrie, discussed the situation and soon, Carrie found a solution to help them shoulder more of their family responsibilities. Clint, was experiencing some of the minor trials of parenthood for the first time.

Karen and Katie, became very aware of how happy their mother was, during that first summer home and they were thrilled for her. She deserved happiness. She had always been so selfless.

They remembered so many times in the past, when she did without so that they could have more. One example that came to mind, was when they were about twelve-years-old they requested a guitar for Christmas, so they could *share* it. Money, as always, was tight. Much to their surprise, on that particular Christmas morning, there were two guitars under the tree. They were delighted!

All of Carrie's children thought she could do the impossible, because somehow she always came through with what they needed. Costumes for plays and Halloween that were too expensive to buy, appeared in the night as they slept.

She could even get a cat's head unstuck from a doorknob hole as children, who were afraid they were in dire trouble, looked on with delight.

* * *

Darla, had memories of a favorite song, which she had loved to sing in her pre-teen years. She had not understood its true meaning in her life and why it meant so much to her. But it became evident after she was grown. The song was "*Scarlet Ribbons.*"

It told of a girl whose desire was for scarlet ribbons for her hair and as she went to sleep, although she still yearned for them, they were not to be found anywhere. It seemed it was just too impossible a dream to come true. Upon waking the next morning, the girl found scarlet ribbons on her bed. Her wish and dream had come true. But, she did not know how. Miraculously they had appeared.

That was just like Carrie. In the night, she would find whatever was needed to make her children's dreams come true. Carrie, was *still* sacrificing for her children, even though they were now adults. She would *always* be a mom. Her children had been her purpose in life...... for so many years and that would never change.

* * *

After a couple of years at college, Katie, who was not quite as *driven* as Karen, was growing unhappy with school and the desire to be a teacher was waning. She decided to drop-out and after trying several different jobs, she returned to Florida to pursue photography. She found a good company to work for and it was there that she met her husband, Sam.

Sam, was a free spirit and Katie's fun loving, relaxed ways proved to be just what he was looking for.

Even though Katie had moved back to Florida to work, she chose to be married at Carrie and Clint's home in Georgia.....with all the trimmings. It would be a small wedding because, for Katie and Sam, money was tight. More importantly, a small informal wedding suited their casual style.

Katie and Carrie, went shopping and they selected a

beautiful, baby blue *southern-belle* dress, with white lace edging the many ruffles. It was on the sale rack and in Katie's price range. Of course, it needed a "quick make over," by Carrie, just in the nick of time. It was perfect!

Katie, looked so pretty with her auburn hair, which she had inherited from her grandfather, Frank. Carrie, brought in ferns and flowers from her yard to decorate the small living-room archway, and the finger sandwiches and wedding cake, baked by Carrie, made the day very special for Katie and Sam. Friends and neighbors became the wedding guests and a local minister, obtained at the last minute, performed the simple ceremony.

As Carrie looked on, she remembered once again how God had blessed her.

One more child had found a mate and Carrie prayed that they would find happiness with each other. She wanted a better life for all her children and if her *prayers* could insure that, then "it was settled."

* * *

Carrie's sons, at this time, had both gone through divorces and financial hard times. They were still desperately trying to get their feet on the ground and the stability of their mother's home was attractive to them. A mother's love never dies.... so Carrie's heart went out to them and she tried to help financially and by giving advice.

Clint, was not happy with the two of them because he felt they took advantage of Carrie and maybe, just a little bit, they reminded him of Oliver. Even so, Clint, soon came to understand that a mother is going to do everything she can to make things better for her children, no matter what they have done or have not done. That was especially true of Carrie.

Later, Clint began to see them through Carrie's eyes and God's eyes and he loved them.

* * *

The next year, Clint retired from his job as a mailman at the local college. The following ten-years flew by with more happiness than Carrie ever thought she would have. Clint, and she were perfect for each other. They each had the same dreams, they had the same values and they went to church *together*. They went out to eat at restaurants and they had friends over. They laughed, talked and shared together.

What made this so remarkable, for Carrie, was the fact that her life with Oliver had been so different. Oliver, never bought Carrie a gift for Christmas or a birthday, never brought her flowers, did not take her out to eat and they did not even have friends over.

Aside from the horse he bought the twins, he had never bought any of the *children* a gift. They never went on a vacation, a trip just for the two of them, or travel as a family. The only trips were to see Oliver's or Carrie's family. That was a vacation to Oliver.

* * *

What a change! Clint, took Carrie to places she had never seen. That was not hard, because she had never been any place except south Alabama and Florida. They criss-crossed the country with friends...... sightseeing and enjoying long, bus-tours with their church group. They saw lovely gardens and historical sights and they loved every minute of their time together.

Clint, had traveled the world in his military career but he, too, was seeing *these* places for the first time.

Life was great and Carrie had to pinch herself every now and then to make sure she was not dreaming.

* * *

Karen, continued to pursue her goal and had recently graduated from college. She was teaching music at a private, Christian school in Florida and it was there she found the young man that would be her husband. Phillip, was also a teacher. He loved musical instruments, as well as singing, and he taught band at the same school.

Darla, Karen's older sister, knew Phillip because they had sung together a few years before, in a singing group representing the local Christian TV station. She could vouch that Phillip was a good choice. Karen, become a part of that same choral group and overtime they fell in love.

Karen's wedding was planned for the next summer. Carrie and Clint, Carrie's daughter Darla, and her granddaughter Jennifer, made the trip to Florida for the big event. The road trip was somewhat stressful and all of them were glad to arrive at their destination. Clint, was *almost* perfect Darla recalled, but she and Jennifer secretly agreed that his driving left *a lot to be desired.* In fact, Darla and Jennifer *both* experienced white-knuckle disease on that trip.

* * *

Carrie, had made Darla's wedding dress *entirely* when she got married, remodeled the blue, ruffled dress for Katie, a day or two before her wedding and now she was putting the *finishing touches* on the hem of Karen's wedding gown.....just minutes before she walked down the aisle.

Darla, and one of the bridegroom's friends were the wedding singers and Karen's twin sister, Katie, was her maid of honor. Aside from the groom's father fainting on stage, during the ceremony, the wedding went off beautifully.

Karen, had become a beautiful young woman and she had found Phillip, a wonderful young man to be her husband. They would continue teaching at the Christian school and set up housekeeping in Florida.

When Karen was married, Carrie had truly cut the tender *everyday* ties with her children. They were all grown now and starting lives of their own.

"God has helped me so much," thought Carrie, as she threw rice and waved goodbye to Karen and Phillip.

"I will pray for you just as I do for the others."

Carrie, was happy and thankful that she had Clint at her side to share these wonderful *family* moments.

* * *

Carrie and Clint, returned to their life in Georgia, but all too soon illness struck their family. Clint, had to have surgery to remove part of his stomach. The surgery was a difficult one, with complications, and took its toll on Clint. His recovery was slow and he was not doing as well as they had hoped. Days turned into weeks, as Carrie sat by his side trying to keep up his spirits.

After a call from Carrie, Darla and John made a trip northward to see them, not knowing what the outcome would be.

Darla's son, Brent, who was in military training at the same base where Clint had served.....training young recruits, also came to visit. They were quite worried because they had never seen Clint look so *sick*. They had always known the tall, handsome Clint, to be strong and vital and this was not like him.

Each time John and Darla come to visit, Clint's unfailing exclamation was.....

"Now, I know I'm going to be alright!"

Those words were repeated many times over the next few years.

He continued to suffer from various illnesses, including hepatitis, which was a result of his days in the military. It culminated two or three years later with the announcement that he had cancer of the liver.

Clint, had two surgeries over the next couple of years, to remove part of the liver.

Finally, after eighteen years of marriage, Carrie heard the words from the doctor that Clint only had a few months to live. She thought she was prepared, but she soon realized that she was not. She loved Clint so much and she kept her fears to herself, trying to encourage him.

Clint, had faith that God would take care of everything and he kept a positive attitude about his illness. His humor and his good nature was not diminished, even by a *serious* illness. And Clint knew, it *was* serious!

Clint, began chemotherapy and fought hard to overcome the cancer. Carrie, prayed constantly for his healing, as did the other family members. He was so sick, but his faith did not wavier.

As Carrie sat by Clint's side, her mind went back to the time when she as a small child, and she heard her own mother pray that a wonderful husband would be spared.....but God had seen fit to answer differently.

"What will God's answer be for me?" Carrie wondered.

* * *

Family reunions were special events. They were cherished times that were enjoyed by all Carrie's children, sons and daughters- in- law, *and* her grandchildren. The last year of Clint's life, as the family gathered in their back yard talking and playing together, Clint called Darla over to the side yard. She could see the serious look on his handsome face. A face she had come to love.

"I want you to take care of your mother," he said softly.

"The house is paid for and if she uses the money right it will last her a long time."

He seemed proud and relieved, that together, they had

been able to save enough money for a comfortable living.

Darla, cringed at the words he spoke. She had heard these words before, when her own father had but a few weeks left to live. But this situation was so different.

"I will," Darla replied, "but you are going to be okay."

"No," Clint said, soft as a whisper.

Darla, could see the resignation in his eyes. There was no fear, just the *knowledge* that comes to those who sense they are reaching the end of their life. He seemed to know, somehow, that this would be *his* last family reunion. These family times had become so important, to both he and Carrie.

Darla, knew this man was her mother's *life* and as she and Clint talked she struggled to keep back the tears. She walked quickly to the kitchen so her mother would not see her tears. Darla had grown close to Clint over the years and thought of him as her father, even *more* than she did her own father.

Clint, had been the one to give advice and show love when she needed it. He was the strong man she could "look up to." He was a man of character and wisdom….. a godly man!

She was saddened at the idea of him not being with them for the *next* family reunion. Soon, Darla wiped her tears and returned to Clint's side, hugging him with a new sense of love. She was hoping to reassure him.

His thoughts were for Carrie and not for himself. That was just like him, such a caring man. He was at peace about his life *and* his God. He was ready to go and his only regret was that he would leave Carrie behind.

* * *

Six months later, Darla and John came to spend the Christmas holidays with Carrie and Clint. You could now see Carrie's personality in the all the furnishings and decorations.

She had long ago made it *their* home. The home where they had lived out *their* love for the last eighteen years.

Memories, of Clint and Millie's life had been packed away in a trunk for years. They would be passed down to Millie's two children, when Clint was gone.

Darla and John, had planned early in the year to spend this Christmas with her mom and Clint. Darla, did not know how things would progress and she wanted to spend every minute their schedules would allow, with them.

* * *

Outings to the mall and eating at their favorite Cafeteria had become a family ritual and on the day after Christmas the four of them kept that tradition.

As they were leaving the cafeteria, Darla and John, and Carrie and Clint walked slowly. Clint, had grown weak physically from the chemo treatments that they hoped and prayed would prolong his life.

Clint's spirit was strong however, and he was still the teaser, joking with people as they walked along the bustling mall corridor. The Christmas decorations were beautiful and people were already out returning their unwanted presents.

"Don't they know that the world is not right?" Darla thought.

"How could they worry about what they got for Christmas, when Clint was dying?"

Darla and Carrie, fell behind in order to talk privately. Carrie, expressed her concern to Darla. Her comments would prove to be true, sooner than either of them could know.

"You never know what this year will hold," she said.

She knew that if God did not choose to heal him, Clint would not last long.

Darla and her sisters, had recently observed that Carrie

needed to get more rest.....if she could. She was looking so tired. But, true to Carrie's nature, she did not concern herself with what she wanted, but with Clint.

"I want to be here for him," she said. "He's been here for me."

And He shall wipe away every tear from their eyes and there shall no longer be any death; there shall no longer be any mourning, or crying or pain...

Rev: 21 4

Chapter Nine

January came...... and the chemo treatments were not able to stop the cancer that ate away at Clint's body. Carrie, called the family to let them know that the end was probably near.

Clint's only brother, who had lived in Alabama, died just a few months before. His mother and father were also gone. Now Carrie's family was *his* family.

Carrie's love and her children's love were now his strength. He was cared for over the last few weeks of his life, by those whom God had given him later in life. Carrie, was not the only one whom God had blessed with a *second chance*.

Clint's last days were sobering as he lay dying and he relived his life, going through the stages of death that they had been told to expect. The most touching was his recount of his military days and especially the times of war.

Darla, Karen and Katie, sat by his side as he *issued orders* to them, just as he had done to his troops. Then he repeated prayers aloud for all to hear. The very same ones that he had prayed over his soldiers and himself, as battles raged, years ago.

On his very last day he asked Carrie to call the minister of his church to come by. He wanted them to sing the songs of faith and hope, that *he* had enjoyed singing so many times before.

God, was his source and even now, it was evident for all to see.

As the songs ended......with Katie, Sam and Carrie by his side, he lifted his hands to the heavens and said,

"I see Him."

"Who do you see?" asked Carrie.

"He is waiting for me."

"I know," Carrie whispered.

"It's okay for you to go with Him. I will come to you again some day."

The words that she had spoken sunk into her heart with dagger-like pain.

Clint, slowly let his hands fall onto the bed and he closed his eyes. He would open them no more.

"I love you 'sugar,'" Clint whispered softly.

"I love you too," replied Carrie..... as she struggled to hold back the tears.

Late that afternoon, with Carrie still by his side, and without regaining consciousness, Clint, breathed one last breath. His strength and his spirit were gone. His body lay still.

Carrie, held him close as she cried aloud. Tears of sorrow and tears of joy mingled down her face as she gave *her love* over to the Lord.

Carrie, forced herself to look into his lifeless face. Here lay the man whom God had given to her. They had shared many good years. They were years she had not expected...... years of wonderful joy. The sorrow was for *her* loss and the joy was for *his* gain.

God, had been good. He had kept His word to bless Carrie for her faithfulness.

* * *

Only two years before, her precious Mama Eva had also died of cancer. Maggie, Hazel, and Carrie, all cared for their mother as she slowly deteriorated from the painful disease.

When Mama Eva died, the whole family felt a big void. Her children, grandchildren and great grandchildren, cherished her and paid loving tribute to her at her funeral. Darla and Karen, had written poems which they read at the funeral.

To Carrie, she was a mother and a faithful friend. However, at that time, Carrie still had Clint to care for her and ease the pain. Now, with *his* passing, it was more than she could bear.

Mama Eva was gone, Oliver was gone, and now Clint, the love of her life was gone. What was she to do?

* * *

Carrie's emotions and mind were numb from the shock of Clint's death. Was he really gone? She could still hear his voice and sense his presence everywhere.

The arrival of friends and family, to offer support and help with funeral arrangements, made the fact abundantly clear. With heavy hearts Carrie's family went through the process of putting their loved one in the ground.

The children, Clint received in the *bargain* when he married Carrie, were there to love him.... even in death. He had been a strong influence in their lives. His Christian character was not a secret to them. He had demonstrated it daily.

The funeral was held on a cold, rainy, February day with a twenty-one-gun salute and military honors. Carrie's face grimaced in pain as she received the flag of the country that Clint had served so well. And with a tearful glance backward, she left *her* Clint in the graveyard, not far from the home where they had shared their life together.

Darla, held Carrie close as she and her mother cried tears of sorrow. Carrie, couldn't help but think of the many times she and Clint had walked there to see the beautiful flowers that adorned the graves. All the seasons were beautiful and in the winter, the sun sparkled on the snow as the colorful flowers fought their way through to create a winter wonderland.

Now Darla and John, Katie and Sam, and Karen, along her daughter Allison, were by their mother's side. Ryan, Brent, and Marcy, three of Darla and John's children, were there along with their families.

Many friends, relatives and neighbors came in support of Carrie and in honor of Clint.

The life that Clint had lived was obvious even in his death. Many people loved and cared for him.

* * *

The day after Clint's funeral, Darla and John, had to leave due to the impending birth of their daughter Jennifer's first child, a little boy. Jennifer's husband, Mike, said that little Alex would have the "best guardian angel," of all. Clint!

One by one…… over the next few days and for various reasons, friends and family left to return to their lives. Carrie, found that she was, once again, *alone.*

She walked the yards that Clint had walked so often. Sat in the metal-spring chair in the little shed, where he had studied God's Word; And she lay nightly in the mahogany spindle bed. The same bed she had risen from, almost nineteen years ago, to make Clint's first breakfast. All these things she found empty, except for the vivid memories she held so tightly in her heart.

Over the next few weeks, Carrie worked with a military representative, who had been assigned to her, to walk her through the mounds of paperwork that needed to be completed because of Clint's death. There was so much to do. Her daughter, Katie, with her husband Sam, was also there to help.

Six months later, she was finished with all the details that follow the death of a spouse or family member. She found herself relieved...... not to have to think about it every day.

Carrie, kept in close touch with her family, but still she felt alone, except for the neighbors and church friends she had enjoyed for many years. She and her friends were all widows now and that created one more special bond between them.

* * *

Over the next few months, Carrie began a downhill slide in her own health. She did not feel well and was not *sure* of herself. She could not make decisions about the small daily things that she had always found easy and she began to doubt herself.

It had been eight months since Clint's death and she felt that she might want to move to Florida to be near her oldest daughter, Darla.

Her brother and sisters, through a series of circumstances over the last few years, now all lived in the same town as Darla.

Carrie, now had no relatives close by..... because Katie and Sam had moved further upstate, due to a job relocation.

She had heard that you should not make any major changes or decisions in your life until one-year had passed, following the death of your spouse. She was one to *follow the rules*, so she delayed one-year and she had "one more" family reunion at her home in May, before she moved back to Florida.

Carrie, arranged to live with Darla and John, just until she could find a home. She was, after all, still very independent!

Darla and John, were happy to have her come and made a room available for her. She had the "run of the house," as she wished.

Soon after Carrie moved in, they began to notice that she was not the same person they had known before Clint's death. She was clumsy, forgetful and overall, she was not sure of herself. She was afraid to go out alone and needed someone to drive her places, although she had her own car.

One day, while at a doctors visit, Darla addressed the situation and it was found.... after some testing, that she was suffering from hypothyroidism which was causing her symptoms.

This was a welcome relief to Carrie and Darla. And shortly after beginning the medication prescribed, Carrie returned to her *old* self.

Another issue that still needed addressing, was the deep grief Carrie was experiencing following Clint's death. Darla, had questioned Carrie about her physical health. She was concerned that she would be okay to move out on her own again. Although she *was* much better, there remained something not yet settled. Darla, again questioned her mother regarding this and it opened up a torrent of tears from Carrie, that were long pent up. Her confession also brought Darla to tears.

"When I married Clint everything was so perfect, everything I had ever dreamed of and when he died, *the dream* died. I miss him so much."

Darla, held Carrie close as she wept. There were no words to take away the pain. She had a hurt that only time would heal.

Carrie, *now realized* that her emotions were frayed..... strongly affected by Clint's death. So....with the discovery of her physical problems, the medications to solve them and the release of grief, she found new hope and strength. Once again, she was ready to build a new life, in a new place near her family and friends.

No one was surprised!

* * *

Finding a house was a first step for Carrie and soon she found the perfect one, that she said, "called her name."

Darla and John, helped her with the closing papers. Carrie's furniture had been in storage and was now brought to her new home. She was making a new beginning in the house that *said* "Carrie," along with *her* memories and *her* hopes, for what remained of her future.

Times with family and friends, old and new, soon became a reality and she had established her life in Florida.

She still had family reunions and family dinners.

She enjoyed playing cards and board games with her sisters and brother.

The yard surrounding her new home was soon full of flowers. It would not be Carrie's home, if it didn't have beautiful flowers.

Her love of the outdoors had not diminished from her childhood days on the farm. The open spaces "called to her and made her feel alive." She loved to see something growing.

* * *

A few weeks after she moved into her new home, Carrie was standing at the sink doing the dinner dishes. She was suddenly jolted from her thoughts when she heard a familiar voice. Carrie, was surprised and sure that she heard Clint's voice at the door. It was so *real* to her that she went looking for him, calling his name. This occurrence, in a strange way, reassured Carrie that Clint knew where she was and approved of her move to be near her family.

Clint, was close in spirit as Carrie lived her life, without him. For many years, she could not keep back the tears as some memory, word, or food would remind her of her deep love for him.

* * *

As the years went by........she began the process of *blending* the lives she had lived with two men......into one life, that belonged to Carrie alone.

Oliver, had given her five children and the wonderful life she had shared with Clint, was such an unexpected blessing. Her life had been a mixture of happiness, hope, pride, love, long suffering and pain..... along with God's blessing.

He had given Carrie, when she was in despair, a *second chance* to know Him.

He had given Oliver a *second chance* to come to Him in his last days..... a miracle in itself. He had given Clint a *second chance* to have the children which he never had.

He had given Clint and Carrie, together, the chance for a special love on this earth. The same love that He desires for everyone to have as a part of their lives.

Even though things were going well, Carrie could not know that life was to drop in her path, yet another obstacle to overcome.....another chance to triumph in the face of difficulty.

Yea though I walk through the valley
of the shadow of death,
I will fear no evil for Thou art with me....

Psalms 23:4

Chapter Ten

Darla, startled by the unexpected ring, sat straight up in bed as John fumbled for the telephone. After a brief moment, still stunned by the interruption of his sleep, John realized it was Carrie. He could tell she was concerned and he quickly handed Darla the phone.

"Hi, it's mom," Darla heard on the other end of the line. Glancing at the clock, Darla could see that it was two o'clock in the morning and her mother would not be calling at that hour unless there was a problem.

"What's wrong?" Darla asked hesitantly.

Carrie, explained the problem she was having and Darla, now wide-awake, dressed quickly and drove to her mom's house across town.

When she arrived, Carrie was having pain......which was growing worse by the minute. Darla, called the paramedics and in a few minutes, they were on the way to the hospital. Darla, drove following close behind the ambulance, wondering what could be wrong with her mother. She was so strong and vital.

Scenes of her mother washing her car, working in her yard and sewing her clothes flashed through her mind.

Darla and John had seen her mom a couple of days before and she was fine. There had been no signs of illness. This was so unexpected.

As Darla reached the hospital, she jumped from her car. Half-walking and half- running, she made her way to the emergency room, where they had taken her mother.

Carrie, was tested for various things, as a process of elimination. Not knowing what was wrong, the doctor decided to keep her overnight.

The next day, Darla received a call from the heart specialist. Her mother had three blocked arteries and needed triple-bypass surgery……or she would not live beyond the next six months.

Darla, immediately called the rest of the family. After much discussion and at the doctors urging, Carrie's surgery was planned for the following day.

* * *

The next few weeks, for Carrie, were a blur of recovery from surgery; A second admission to the hospital for fluid retention in the lungs, which was a complication of surgery; Then, a third admission for severe nosebleeds……all of which drained Carrie of her will to live. She had *had it* and she wished to die.

She made her daughter, Darla, promise that she would not do anything else to help her live, if she had more problems. Darla herself, was drained from all the events and caring for her mother.

However, through the encouragement of her family and many prayers, Carrie recovered from the physical problems. But it was not over. Through a series of bad experiences at the hospital, Carrie was left with a different kind of wound…….a trauma that you could not see. Anxiety attacks became the next major obstacle that she would have to work through...but she made it!

This illness was another opportunity for Carrie to display her strong determination. Each day, she demonstrated the hope and faith that had carried her through many situations in her life.

She learned, yet again, that God is the God of *second chances!* He, is the provider for all of our needs. We are all important to him.

* * *

"So......who is Carrie?"

She, was a little girl brought up in the depression years......who struggled through a rough marriage and raised five children..... with little earthly help!

She is the one with a husband who found the Lord when most thought there was no hope.

Carrie, is the one that God blessed with the "love of her life," as a reward for faithfulness. She has a good life with friends and family that love her even today.

She has been blessed with long life!

Over the years, Carrie passed down her singing, sewing and decorating abilities to her three daughters, Darla, Karen, and Katie. To her grand-daughter-in-law, Dana, the art of quilting. To her children, grandchildren and great-grandchildren, she passed down stories of her life on the farm...... in the days of the great depression, as well as the work ethic that she learned over many years.

To her two sons, Foster and Loren, she passed along all the love and support she could give and she loves them for *who* they are, not for *what* they have accomplished.

* * *

Carrie, made wrong choices and mistakes along the way.

But we can see through her life, that even though we fail, God is there to help us and keep us from destruction.

With God's help, Carrie has developed a life for herself....here and now. But she never forgets the life she *has* lived and the things that shaped her life along the way.

* * *

Following her recovery from heart surgery, at age eighty-two, she is again planting her flowers, washing her car, keeping her house and remodeling her bathroom.

The values instilled in her, by Mama Eva and Papa Ed, as a child on the farm still prevail. She squeezes a penny, gives her opinion freely, and she loves her family greatly. Wal-Mart is *her* store.

She prays for *all* her family and wonders, as Mama Eva did before her, why she is still here with us...... ten years after Clint's death. Obviously, we need her.

Her house is still *the gathering place*!

Who can find a virtuous woman?...... her price is far above rubies ......the heart of her husband doeth safely trust in her......let her works praise her in the gates ...... her children rise up and call her blessed....

Proverbs 31

The story goes on....

The last chapter of Carrie's life cannot be written...... she has more to do.

Her family loves her, depends on her and they have hope of many years to come...... sharing with her...... benefiting from her prayers.

What did that little girl who made wrong choices accomplish?

A life well spent is what Carrie has accomplished. She, like most of us, has not risen to worldwide fame and not many people even know her. Only her children, her friends and her relatives know her value.

Well, that is not true...... God knows her......and He knows her best. He has blessed her "here and now," and He will bless her in the life to come.

Her children rise up and call her blessed!

* * *

Carrie,

You have done well! You have given us the same unmovable hope that brought you through many of life's trials and problems. The same hope that kept you faithful and "on track," as you experienced the "road of life"...... through the years.

Your determination and goodness have prevailed. Your value we cannot measure and surely, your reward will be great in heaven!

* * *

Thank You God! You are the God of second chances!

Printed in the United States
42269LVS00004B/21

9 781597 812375